"Hey you, man. Where you from?"

Everyone stared at Amir. I felt sorry for him. It's hard being the new person. He should've walked home some other way, I thought. Amir looked at Sherman.

"Same place you from," he said. We laughed.

"No you not. 'Cause you ain't as fine as me."

Everyone laughed again. Amir laughed, too. I was surprised. If Sherman had said that to me, I'd been real mad at him. I thought Sherman was warming up and getting ready to put a name on Amir. But he didn't say nothing else. He just seemed to get in a good mood.

And when Sherman, Big Russell and the other boys walked over to the park to practice some basketball, Amir went with them, like, as my grandmother would say, it was something he'd been doing every day of his life.

THE GIFT-GIVER

THE GIFT-GIVER

JOYCE HANSEN

CLARION BOOKS
New York

To My Mother and Father

Clarion Books
a Houghton Mifflin Company imprint
215 Park Avenue South, New York, NY 10003
Copyright © 1980 by Joyce Hansen

For information about permission to reproduce selections from this book, write to Permissions, Houghton Mifflin Company, 215 Park Avenue South, New York, NY 10003.

www.houghtonmifflinbooks.com

Printed in the U.S.A.

The Library of Congress has catalogued the hardcover edition as follows:

Hansen, Joyce. The gift-giver.
Summary: The year she is in fifth grade, Doris meets a special friend in her Bronx neighborhood.
[1. Friendship—Fiction. 2. Afro-Americans—Fiction.]
I. Title. PZ7.H19825Gi   1980   [Fic]   80-12969

                              CL ISBN-10: 0-395-29433-9
PA ISBN-13: 978-0-618-61123-2   PA ISBN-10: 0-618-61123-1

MP 25 24 23 22 21 20

Contents

·1·

Spring Fever

Yellow Bird was on the window ledge; Russell crunched a big lollipop; Mickey and Dotty raised their hands. Mrs. Brown asked Sherman to name the fiftieth state and he said he didn't remember but he could name the fifty-first. And Amir looked at all of us like we was crazy.

I felt sorry for Amir. It was hard to come to our fifth-grade class in April. We'd all been together since last year—me, Yellow Bird, Big Russell, Mickey and Dotty, Sherman and the rest. I took one look at Amir and knew he'd have a hard time.

First, he'd have to get a name. Like we call Yellow Bird, Yellow Bird 'cause he's little and pale and got a long beakish nose. And we call Big Russell, Big Russell 'cause he's big. But we also call him Big Hocks behind his back; everybody's afraid to say that to his face. We like Big Russell but we careful how we call him.

And Mickey and Dotty—the twins. They was borned with them names. It fit them so good nobody bothered to give them new ones. Mickey and Dotty don't look

1

exactly alike. Dotty is so short she looks like a little round dot. Mickey is a little taller than Dotty. But you can be taller than Dotty and still be short.

So when this new boy Amir came I tried to think of a name for him. But Sherman was the namer. When Sherman named you that was your name for good.

I pulled Mickey's sleeve. "What you think Sherman is going to call that new boy?" I asked.

"He looks peculiar, don't he?" she said.

"Look at them big, shining brown eyes. He's little and skinny too."

"Maybe they'll call him Light Bulbs or Mr. Watts," Mickey laughed.

I felt like a big, old hunk of a girl when I looked at him. Mrs. Brown stared at me, her face made up like she had eaten some bad-smelling thing. I wondered whether she was still on the fifty states.

"Doris, I'm going to contact your mother. You've played and talked the entire fifth grade away."

Yellow Bird saved me. Mrs. Brown saw him on the ledge and dashed to the window. Then the bell rang. And you know what happened. Everybody scrambled to the closets. Everybody except Amir. He just sat there, his eyes big and shining. Mrs. Brown held poor Yellow Bird by the collar.

"That boy must really think he a bird—sitting out on that ledge," said Sherman.

Everyone laughed. Mrs. Brown looked swelled up like a balloon. She let out a scream that must a been heard straight down to the principal's office. We was used to her swelling up and screaming, but this time she sounded like she busted something inside herself.

2

We got quiet, sat down and took our pencils and notebooks.

"School's not over for this class. Your behavior has been horrendous this afternoon."

Nobody said boo. Sherman remembered what the fiftieth state was; Big Russell finished his lollipop and copied the notes; Yellow Bird named the thirteen original colonies; Mickey and Dotty kept their hands down and Amir had a little smile around his mouth as he sat with his hands folded. He'd already copied his notes and answered five questions correctly. I wondered how he knew the answers, being this was his first day in our class.

When we finished, Mrs. Brown fussed some more and let us go. No one said a thing until we got out in the street. Then Sherman started.

"I'm gonna make that Mrs. Brown wish she never heard of Sherman Shepard. Why all them Black teachers got to be so strict?"

"We only got two at Dunbar," I said.

"It's a good thing. Otherwise our butts be worked to death."

As we walked down 163rd Street, Sherman looked around like he missed something. He grinned.

"Hey you, man. Where you from?"

Everybody stared at Amir. I felt sorry for him. It's hard being the new person. He should've walked home some other way, I thought. Amir looked at Sherman.

"Same place you from," he said. We laughed.

"No you not. 'Cause you ain't as fine as me."

Everyone laughed again. Amir laughed too. I was surprised. If Sherman had said that to me I'd been real mad at him. I thought Sherman was warming up and getting ready to put a name on Amir. But he didn't say nothing else. He just seemed to get in a good mood.

And when Sherman, Big Russell and the other boys walked over to the park to practice some basketball, Amir went with them, like, as my grandmother would say, it was something he'd been doing every day of his life.

·2·

Naming

I looked at Mickey and Dotty. They were strutting behind the boys.

"Where y'all going?" I yelled.

Mickey turned around. "To the playground. We don't
feel like going straight home. Come on."

"I gotta go home."

"Why?"

"You know I gotta go straight home from school."

"You can't do nothing. Your mama treat you like a big,
old baby."

Mickey knew I hated her to say that. "I can do anything anybody else does," I said.

"You can't do nothing."

"You need to mind your business, Mickey. I do what
I want. I've seen your mother run you and Dotty in the
house."

"Yeah, but we don't get run in the house much as you
do," Dotty said.

"I'll show you. Let's go to the playground," I said. I'll
worry about what my mother's gonna say later, I thought

to myself. I was tired of them laughing at me 'cause I couldn't do nothing. Anyway I didn't want to miss Sherman putting a name on Amir.

The boys took their positions on the basketball court. Amir stood by the fence. Someone said to him, "Hey, man. You want to play?"

"No, I'll watch."

"You gonna see a lot with them big eyes."

What he come here for if he not going to play ball, I wondered. Sherman, with his long, skinny self and his big Afro, spun and danced around the court. He shouted orders to everyone. Mickey looked up at me.

"Is Sherman the coach?" she asked.

Big Russell almost squashed Yellow Bird. It seemed like they forgot about Amir. Mickey looked like she was interested in the practice. Dotty looked 'cause that's what Mickey did.

After a while I said, "Later Mickey, I'm going on home. Nothing happening around here." Soon as I said that the boys stopped playing.

Amir walked over to a bench and sat down. Me and Mickey and Dotty walked over to the bench too. I talked to Mickey—trying to act like we was having a serious conversation—like we didn't realize we was walking to the benches—and didn't know the boys was there. Amir smiled at us. Then Sherman and Big Russell came over.

"Here it comes now," I said.

"Here comes what?" asked Mickey.

"That new boy gonna get a name."

"He already got a name."

"Mickey, you don't understand nothing."

Sherman sat next to Amir and looked at him like he

never saw him before. Amir looked right back at him. Sherman reared back and covered his eyes like when you get blinded by the sun. They all laughed. Amir didn't smile. But he didn't look mad or scared either. Sherman's eyes got small and all sparkly.

He's gonna come out with a good one now, I said to myself.

Sherman said, "Why you so quiet, man? Are you strange or something?"

"Yeah," someone yelled, "he the stranger."

"Is there any more like you at home?" someone else said.

"Do you have a home?"

They laughed like they really said something funny.

Sherman had a devilish look in his eyes. "Where you get that name from?" he asked. "What does it mean?"

Amir stood up. "My mother and father gave me my name. Who gave you yours?"

Sherman leaned back. His spaghetti legs dangled all over the bench. "What you standing up for, man? You gonna knock me out or something?"

I don't know why, but suddenly I was sorry I was there. Amir looked so little and lonely. Mickey and Dotty acted like they was watching their favorite TV show.

Yellow Bird tuned up his lips to say something, when T.T., this old frowsy boy from Union Avenue, got into the act too.

"Say, you don't play no ball? What's wrong with you?"

"I like to watch," Amir said, looking him dead in the eye.

"Why? You can't play? Or you think you too good to play with us?"

Sherman turned to T.T. "As bad as you play who want to play with you?"

Then Big Russell got into it. "Yeah, T.T. Maybe you should watch too. Maybe you learn something."

"Listen, Hocks, I'm gonna bring my boys over here and show you 163rd Street clowns how to play some ball."

Now like I said before, no one ever called Russell Big Hocks to his face—no one except someone crazy like T.T. Russell flew off the bench and T.T. dashed out the park. All the boys followed, yelling and laughing. They forgot about Amir. Mickey and Dotty followed the boys like two little tails. I was glad they all left.

Me and Amir walked without talking, back to 163rd Street. I wanted to speak to him, but I couldn't get the words to come out right. I wanted to ask him why he went to the playground in the first place. Why didn't he just run home and stay in the house the way all kids do when they first come to a new school or move to a new neighborhood? Why did he hang around and wait right there for somebody to bother him? And I wanted to ask why he didn't try to act like the other boys if he was going to hang out with them. But we got to Amir's building before I could figure a way to say all that.

Anyway, I had more important things to worry about. It was late and Mama was upstairs steaming. I didn't even have time to think up a good reason for not coming straight home.

All this trouble for nothing. Amir didn't even get a name.

8

·3·

Under Punishment

"Girl, why you so late from school?"

"I went to the library."

"I don't see no library books."

"I read there."

She had little pieces of chopped meat on her hands. We gonna have them meat balls again, I said to myself.

"Doris, you gonna be punished twice. Once for lying and once for not coming straight home. Now where you been?"

"I went to the playground with Mickey and Dotty because the. . . ."

She whomped me across the face before I finished. I yelled.

"Shut up that noise 'fore I give you something to cry about. You better wash them dishes in the sink. And make your bed. I told you about leaving the house without making your bed. And I told you about that playground. You a hard head child. Shut up that noise 'fore you wake the baby."

I felt like doing something crazy. Like dashing out the house and running away. Everybody be looking for me. Mama be crying and begging me to come home. But I wouldn't come back till I got good and ready! Maybe I wouldn't come back till I was twenty-one years old—I'd have a good job making lots of money. Mama wish she'd been nicer to me.

And Mickey and Dotty be sorry they laughed at me. They'd be jealous when they saw how good I was doing.

I put my books down and peeped out the kitchen window. Mickey and them ran through the alley. They'd be out till seven or eight. I was in for good and it was only four-thirty. I started washing the dishes. I had eight years before I'd be eighteen and free. Eight years was a long time. I'd probably be hit by a truck or die of pneumonia before I was twelve.

I felt like breaking every dish. Mama came in the kitchen. I'd be nagged some more. I couldn't say boo else I'd get whacked again.

"Someday you gonna appreciate me and your daddy. Kids be messing with drugs. And them gangs is always fighting in that playground. It ain't no place for a little girl."

Little girl, I thought. I'm almost tall as she is. I couldn't say nothing. When she believed something, nobody could change her mind except my father—sometimes.

Nobody came around us with no drugs in that playground. And people was always saying there was going to be a gang fight. We never saw gang the first. The one time there was a gang fight was at night.

Sometimes them Union Avenue boys be drinking that sneaky pete wine, that's all. I was glad when she told me to get the baby. At least I wouldn't hear no more lectures. The baby—Gerald—is one year old. Sometimes I like him. But most times he gets on my nerves. I have to be rocking him when I could be doing something else.

Soon as my father walked in the door she told him. He didn't say anything all through dinner. But I knew it was coming. Daddy never allowed us to talk about problems while we ate. He'd say it was bad for the digestion.

I walked into the living room and looked out the window. Sherman and Russell was still outside playing. I heard Daddy come into the room, but I stared out the window, like I didn't notice him. The big, ragged leather chair scrunched when he sat down. I still made believe I didn't notice him.

"Come here, Doris."

I took a chance and didn't answer.

"Doris!" He said it fast and loud. I knew I'd better look like I heard him.

"Come over here, girl."

I went over to him. I figured they'd put me under punishment and make me stay in the house. They acted like it's the worst thing they could do to me. I thought about making them think I wanted to stay in the house all the time, then they'd send me outside for punishment.

"Doris, me and your mother decided that you'll be under punishment all week. You can't play outside after your homework. Can't go to the movies Saturday. You got to learn to come straight home after school, like you told."

At first I didn't say anything. Then I remembered that the next day was the big basketball game between the fifth and sixth grades. I'd picked the worst time to mess up.

"Daddy, tomorrow is the big game after school. Can I stay for that?"

"They gonna miss you this year," my mother hollered from the kitchen.

I hated when she did that. It was like her ears was all over the house. She could hear everything anyone said or did. You couldn't escape her ears—or her mouth.

"But I been looking forward to this game all year," I said to my father.

The voice came from the kitchen again. "You should've thought of that before you decided to take yourself over to that playground. You already had your after-school fun."

My father spoke real soft. "Doris, I'm sorry. You have to come straight home from school."

"She's the one who should be saying sorry," my mother yelled. "A hard head makes a soft behind."

I think my father was surprised she heard him. He was really trying to talk soft.

I whispered, "Daddy, please, I'll stay under punishment from now till June, but please, don't make me miss the game."

Ma came flying into the room. Guess I whispered lower than she could hear. She couldn't stand that.

"Look Doris, we already told you. You coming straight home from school," she said.

"Mama, please. I promise I'll do anything you say. Please let me go to the game."

"No, and that's it. You got to learn to do what you told."

"Why is this game so important, Doris?" my father asked.

"It's between the fifth and sixth grades. Looks like we're going to win this time. Please Daddy?"

My mother stood there with her arms folded around a dish towel. "Who on that team? That rude, skinny Sherman? And that tub-a-lard Russell? That who you want to see? What you should be doing is reading some books after school—getting something in your head."

"Ma, why you hate Russell and them?"

"I don't hate them. They somebody's children just like you my child. And I hope their mamas be telling them the same thing I'm telling you—to get something in their heads."

My father sat there quiet. I tried to read his face, but I couldn't tell what he was thinking. I decided to start crying. I knew that'd get to him.

My mother rolled her eyes at me. "Stop that, Doris."

Then my father looked at me, but he talked to my mother. "Let her go to the game," he said. "Nothing else."

My mother has kind of slanty eyes. When she gets mad they look like two black slits. I turned to my father. "Daddy, please?"

This time he looked at my mother. "Just let her go to the game. She'll come home right after."

Mama sucked her teeth real loud and stomped into the kitchen. She clanged and banged pots and pans like it was New Year's Eve. Then the baby started crying. It looked like I saw a laugh somewhere in my father's face. "Doris, stop crying," he said. "Go and get the baby. This sounds like a crazy house."

13

I was miserable for the rest of the night. When I went to bed I heard them talking. My ears ain't like my mother's so I couldn't tell what they was saying. But I decided there was no way I was gonna miss that game. I'd go anyway. Since I was already under punishment, there'd just be some more punishment added to that. Probably I'd get a whipping. Still, I couldn't miss the game for nothing in the world.

When I got to the kitchen the next morning my father had already left for work. Mama was still banging pots. Sometimes I felt sorry for those pots and pans. I didn't say nothing. I just drank my milk.

"Listen, Miss, you speak when you come in this kitchen."

"Mornin'," I said quietly.

"You lucky your father is so soft-hearted. He talked me into letting you stay after school for the game."

"Oh, Ma!" I yelled so loud the baby jumped.

"Okay, all that noise ain't necessary."

She came over to me and shook her finger in my face. "Girl, you better walk a straight line home after that game."

·4·

The Game

The first crazy thing about that day was that Sherman was absent. This was the day of the big basketball game between the fifth and sixth grades. Sherman was the captain of the fifth-grade team. Big Russell was angry because of Sherman. I was mad too. We just knew that the fifth grade would win this year 'cause Sherman was so good.

As usual we went to the schoolyard after lunch. Amir came with us—quiet like always. All the boys practiced for the game except Big Russell. He sat by himself looking like a fat volcano ready to explode. We all knew to stay away from him when he got mad. Russell is okay but you always got to be so careful how you act with him. I went over to him, kind of nervous-like. Amir followed me.

"Russell, what you think happened to Sherman?" I asked.

"How I know? He just don't care, I guess."

15

"Maybe he's sick," I said.

"He ain't sick. He just don't care about us winning."

Amir turned to Russell. "Don't you know how to play basketball?"

Lordy, I said to myself. This boy better stop asking Russell them dumb questions.

Russell looked at Amir like he was crazy. "Of course, man. What you ask me that for? You trying to be funny?"

"Since you play too, why you thinking you'll lose 'cause Sherman ain't here?"

"Don't you understand nothing? Sherman is the captain. He's the best player, man. He plays better than them sixth graders. He tall and big like them."

"So are you," said Amir.

Oh, oh, I said to myself. Russell gonna bust him a good one now if he don't shut up.

But Russell just looked at Amir again, like Amir had no sense at all.

"Sherman knows all the moves. All the plays," he said.

"Don't you know them too?" Amir asked.

"Yeah, but he's the captain. We need another man. None of them guys is good as Sherman."

"Use Yellow Bird," Amir said.

Even I had to laugh at that. Yellow Bird never played in important games. I mean it was crazy to think of Yellow Bird with his little, short self trying to play a regular game with guys like Russell and Sherman—not to mention those big sixth graders.

"You really stupid, man. Bird can't play in no regular game!" Russell yelled.

"He practices with you. He's little and fast and could keep the other team confused."

"Look, Amir, you're confused. It don't make no

16

difference. We gonna lose anyway. I'm gonna get Sherman good for this."

"If you gonna lose anyway, may as well put Yellow Bird in the game."

Russell looked at Amir like he was really gonna hit him this time.

"Man, what do you know? You can't even play ball."

At three o'clock everyone headed for the gym. We looked forward to this game all year. The fifth grade had never beat the sixth grade at Paul Laurence Dunbar Elementary School. I felt real bad for the team 'cause they thought they had a chance this time. This was the one time I hoped Big Russell would get Sherman for letting everyone down like this.

Me and Mickey and Dotty got good seats in front. I saw Amir on the other side of the court talking to Big Russell. I wanted to know so bad what they said my ears hurt.

"Hey, Mickey, I wonder what them boys talking about."

"About the game."

"I know that. But what they saying?"

"How should I know?"

"Tell Dotty to go over there and find out."

We always sent Dotty on errands to find out what people said. Somehow she could be some place and nobody see her. She came back in two minutes, sat down and didn't say a thing.

"What them boys saying?" I asked.

"That new boy just say 'You play good like Sherman, you should win.'"

"That sound like some of that Amir talk. What Big Russell say?"

17

"My mama don't allow me and Mickey to talk like that."

Sometimes I don't understand Dotty at all. What did her mama have to do with her telling me what them boys said? Before I could ask her to explain, the game started.

The sixth-grade team came out first and them old sixth graders in the audience yelled and hollered. I got so mad. They knew they was gonna win.

Then the fifth-grade team came out. Russell led them. Suddenly the audience started stomping and yelling. I looked to see what the noise was about. Who do I see at the end of the lineup but Yellow Bird, looking like he wearing his daddy's drawers.

Russell went and listened to Amir after all. Yellow Bird was a sight. Even me and Mickey and Dotty laughed until our faces hurt. Yellow Bird didn't care. He grinned and got ready to act the fool. At least we had a good laugh even if we lost the game.

The game began. First of all, I thought Yellow Bird was going to lose them shorts he was wearing. That kept me worried. Them shorts waved like flags as he flew from one end of the court to the other.

Russell looked like a tank—mowing people down.

The sixth graders had six points and the fifth graders six fouls. Then I heard some noise on the other side of the gym.

I see Amir moving around where a lot of fifth graders is sitting. Then he comes running over to me and Mickey and Dotty. He puts them big eyes on me and says, "We cheering for Russell."

So we all yelled, "Go, Russell! Go Russell!" Seemed like every fifth grader was yelling.

Meanwhile, down on the court, Russell is butting heads and Bird is flapping. But Russell made a basket and finally got them two points.

Bird caught the ball and spun like a top back to Russell who made a beautiful hook shot.

The fifth-grade team started moving. Yellow Bird darted and dribbled all over the place. No one could catch him.

Russell made all kinds of shots.

The sixth-grade team looked confused. Another point for the fifth grade. Then the crowd starts yelling, "Go Bird! Go Russell!" We screamed till we lost our voices.

It was worth it. For the first time in the history of Dunbar Elementary, the fifth-grade basketball team beat the sixth grade. They beat them just by one point. But that didn't matter.

Of course, Bird and Russell was the stars. Russell looked like he lost twenty pounds 'cause he wasn't blown up and evil anymore. He looked so proud it made me feel proud.

Before I even had a chance to say something about the game to her, Mickey was on the court grinning in Yellow Bird's face. Dotty disappeared too. I remembered I was under punishment. I left without saying anything to anybody. I didn't want everyone to know I had to leave right away.

I walked down 163rd Street slow as I could and still keep moving. I saw Amir and caught up to him. After I ran over to him I felt stupid. I didn't know what to say. He looked at me and smiled.

"That was some game," he said.

"Yeah. The fifth grade did good." I wanted to ask him

something about himself. But how you ask somebody why they strange?

"Hey, Amir, how come you. . . ."

Some boys from our class came dashing down the street. "Amir. Come on to the playground with us."

Amir looked at me. "See you later, Doris."

He went with the other boys. Mickey and Dotty came over to me. "Let's go to the playground," they said.

"I gotta do some things for my mother."

They laughed. "Come on, Dotty," Mickey said. "Let's find Lavinia or anybody who can do something."

"You some friends," I yelled to them. They just laughed again.

I went upstairs. Mama still looked mad. But she was baking a chocolate cake—my favorite, and this wasn't even Sunday. I went to my room which was really a hallway. But it was my own spot.

"Get the baby, Doris. Don't you hear him crying?"

Don't you hear me crying? I thought. I'm never going to get married or have babies. I'm going to be free and do everything I want.

I thought about Amir. If I could've went to the playground I could've talked to him. When I picked up the baby he started crying even more. I felt like crying too.

All I wanted was to do some of the things my friends did. Mickey and Dotty was my best friends, but I could tell they was getting tired of being with me 'cause I couldn't do anything.

·5·

Missing

The next morning I waited for Mickey and Dotty, but they never showed up. I took the shortcut through the playground. Mama said I couldn't play in the playground. She didn't say I couldn't use it as a shortcut to get to school. I saw Mickey and Dotty up ahead and ran over to them.

"Hey, I waited for you this morning. What happened?"

Dotty didn't even bother to answer. Mickey said, "We thought your mother wouldn't let you come out."

"You think you so funny! You could've waited for me."

Dotty twisted her little round head to the side. "Me and Mickey thought you was gone. Lots of times you don't wait for us, you know!"

"That's a lie! I always wait."

"You better not call my sister a liar," Mickey said.

Dotty twisted her face. "Come on, Mickey," she said. "Forget her."

"Later for both of you," I said.

I walked away from them. I should've known when

I saw them dressed exactly alike in green skirts and green sweaters that they was gonna be acting hinkty. It was sickening having twins for friends anyway. Sometimes they act like nobody's in the world but them.

When I got near the school I saw Amir.

"What's wrong with you this morning?" he asked.

"Nothing."

"You look mad."

"I ain't mad."

"You walking fast like you're mad. Where's your two friends?"

"What friends?"

"The twins."

"We ain't really friends. We just acquaintances."

He started looking around the schoolyard. "I wonder if Sherman is in school today."

"Who cares?" I said.

"Russell, Yellow Bird—everybody cares."

"He didn't care enough about us to show up for the game."

"Maybe he's sick."

"Maybe. Maybe not."

He looked around and saw Russell and them in the yard. "I'll see you later, Doris."

Soon as he left I felt a little bad about the way I talked to him, but he didn't act like he was insulted.

It was good I didn't have them twin friends anymore. That day was the first time all year I didn't get in trouble for talking in class.

Everybody else was still excited about the game. Mickey and Dotty got a pass to the bathroom and stayed an hour.

Russell autographed basketballs instead of copying notes off the board.

Yellow Bird came flying in the room playing basketball with big wads of paper. Of course, Amir behaved.

And Sherman still wasn't back.

We went to the yard at lunchtime. There was a whole crowd of kids around Bird and Russell.

"Hey, Bird, play some ball with us after school."

"Russell, you made some nice moves yesterday."

"Bird, you got to show me some of that."

"Come around the block after school."

And that Mickey and Dotty was twitching and dancing around Bird and Russell too.

People sure is phony, I thought. They used to laugh in Bird's face and behind Big Russell's back, now they was all over them.

Suddenly someone yelled, "Hey, there goes Sherman."

"Sherman!" Russell shouted.

Sherman just looked in the yard and then turned around and ran. Everybody ran out the yard calling him. Amir was the only boy who stayed. He sat down on the school steps and I walked over to him.

"How come you didn't run after Sherman too?" I asked.

"Sherman don't want to talk to no one."

"How you know?"

"I could tell. He didn't run 'cause he was scared. He just don't want to be bothered."

I sat down next to Amir. "Yeah, I was thinking the same thing. I told you that boy just don't care about nobody. I knew he wasn't sick."

"Maybe he's in trouble."

"He just playing hookey and acting crazy," I said.

Amir didn't say nothing else. He just looked real quiet and serious.

"Hey, Amir, how come you . . . I mean, why did you . . . How come you don't act like you just moved here?"

He looked at me a long time and I felt kind of stupid. Then he smiled a little. "I'm used to moving to different schools. And new neighborhoods."

"How come you just followed Sherman and them to the park the other day? You know they was going to bother you."

He shrugged his shoulders. "They would bother me more if I ran home scared. It's better to face it and get it over with. Now we friends. You ever move to a new block or a new school?"

"Nope. I been living on 163rd Street all my life."

I was sorry when the bell rang to go back in. I saw Russell and them running back to the school. I wondered if they caught up with Sherman.

When we got out of school that afternoon Mickey and Dotty ignored me and I ignored them. Russell and the other boys disappeared before I could ask them about Sherman. I walked real slow hoping I might see Amir, but he was gone too.

Just as I started going into my building I heard him calling me.

"Doris, I was looking for you. Where you went so fast after school?"

Here I was walking like a turtle so I could see him and he's talking about where I went so fast.

"I heard that Sherman's family moved," he said.

"Russell and them talked to him?"

"No, they didn't catch up to him. Lavinia told me."

Lavinia is the most gossipy girl in our class.

"How she know?" I asked.

"She said that's what she heard."

"She always hearing something. How come he ain't tell nobody good-bye?"

"That's what I asked her."

"I saw his grandmother yesterday," I said.

"Did she say good-bye?"

"That mean old woman never talks to no one."

Amir sat on the bannister. "You going upstairs now?" he asked.

"Yeah."

"I'll see you tomorrow then." He left the stoop and ran toward the playground.

At least he didn't act like I was a freak because I had to go in the house.

As I ran up the stairs to my apartment I thought about Sherman. He had about eight brothers and sisters. There was so many of them that you always saw somebody from that family. But come to think of it, I hadn't seen none of them for the past two days. I only saw his grandmother, and like I said before, she never talks.

Next day at lunchtime I heard five different rumors about Sherman. I wondered whether Lavinia started all of them.

One boy said Sherman was sent to reform school. A girl in class 6–1 said he was just playing hookey.

Another girl said she heard he was scared Big Russell would beat him up for missing the game. I guess Big Russell started that rumor.

Another boy said he heard Sherman was suspended from school, but he didn't know why.

Me and Mickey and Dotty still wasn't talking to each

other, even though we was standing around in the schoolyard listening to the same rumors. I noticed that this day
the twins wasn't dressed exactly alike.

Suddenly Dotty goes over to some little fourth graders
and starts jumping double-dutch with them.

Then Amir says that maybe we should go to Sherman's
house and find out what really happened.

Mickey says, "Yeah. That's what we should do." Then
she looks at me. I made believe I didn't see her and
turned to Amir.

"No one goes to his house," I said.

"That's right. His grandmother hates kids. And they
can't have no company," Mickey said. She looked at me
again like she was talking to me. I looked back at her,
but I really didn't want to.

"Yeah. No one goes there," I said.

The bell rang and I walked back to the building.
Mickey followed me. Dotty was still jumping double-
dutch like a little nut.

"That's really something about Sherman," she said.

"No one knows what happened." I walked real fast,
but she kept following me.

"You think he afraid of Big Russell?" she asked in a
little whiney voice.

"Girl, you crazy. Sherman could beat that fat Russell
into a Virginia ham," I said.

We laughed so hard we couldn't stop. When we got
to the room Mrs. Brown made up her face right away.

"Shut up that racket. You've been so good for the past
two days, Doris. Don't spoil it."

School was long and hot and boring that afternoon.
But everytime me and Mickey looked over at Russell we
had to cover our mouths to keep from laughing.

Then Mrs. Brown called Russell up to the board. Mickey drew a picture of a big ham and showed it to me. We tried not to laugh out loud. But we couldn't help it. Me and Mickey exploded. We was all doubled over laughing and crying.

Mrs. Brown stopped her lesson. "Mickey and Doris, go and stand in the hall until you control yourselves."

We went outside. When we looked at each other we started laughing. I guess you could say we was friends again.

After school Mickey and Dotty headed for the playground and I went home.

For the rest of the week all we heard was these stories about Sherman. By the time the weekend came I was off punishment, but it didn't matter 'cause it rained all weekend. I still had to stay in the house because of the rain, so I didn't hear any news about Sherman.

·6·

Runaway

On Monday morning me and Mickey and Dotty took the shortcut through the playground to school. As we passed the swings we saw Sherman sitting by himself on a bench. Before we could say hello, he just got up and ran. "What's wrong with him?" Mickey said.

"That boy is going crazy. Running from us like he's scared."

I told Amir and Big Russell when we was all walking back home from school what happened. Russell said, "That's what he did last week. And I saw him this morning too and he did the same thing to me. Guess he scared I'm going to get him for missing the game."

I said to myself, You know good and well Sherman ain't afraid of you.

"Something must've happened to him," Amir said.

"Like what? He just afraid, that's all," Russell answered.

"Is he afraid of me and Mickey and Dotty too? He ran from us."

Russell looked at me. "As ugly as you girls is, who wouldn't run from you?"

All the boys started laughing. Sometimes I hated Big Russell. He was so mean. Amir was the only boy who didn't laugh.

Dotty put her hands on her hips and stuck out her mouth. "You a big, fat hog, Big Hocks."

She flew down the street and me and Mickey went right behind her.

When we got to Mickey and Dotty's stoop I said, "Dotty, why you say that to him? Now he's going to bother us all week long."

Russell never hit girls, but he'd tease you, pull on you and embarrass you in front of everybody. We was in for a miserable week. I sat on Mickey and Dotty's stoop. "Now I can't even go back home until Russell leave my stoop."

"We going upstairs now," Mickey said.

"See how dirty y'all are? I got to go back over to my building with that Big Russell on the stoop and you and Dotty is safe in your house."

"Big Russell ain't gonna bother you. See you later."

Dotty just kept popping her gum and acting like she didn't even care. Sometimes I think that girl ain't got sense enough to be afraid of nobody. Not even Big Russell.

When they left I heard someone from down in the basement calling my name. I looked over the railing and saw Sherman sitting outside the basement door on a box.

"What you doing down there?"

"Shush. I don't want no one to know I'm here."

"Why you been running from people?"

"I don't want no one to know my business."

"What business?"

"I ran away."

"You ain't go far. Your family is in the next building."

"I ain't run from there. I ain't got no more family. They broke us up."

"What're you talking about? They who?"

"The authorities. They say my grandma too old to take care of us, so they put us in different homes."

"You mean with other people in your family?"

"No, with strangers. In a foster home."

"Foster home? Where your brothers and sisters?"

"We all in different homes."

I never heard about things like foster homes before. "Where's your mother and father?"

"I ain't got none." He looked like he was gonna cry so I didn't say nothing else. I thought everyone had a mother and father.

"I ran away from the foster home. I hate it. Nobody can make me stay there."

"Why don't you go back to your grandma?"

" 'Cause that's the first place they'll look for me. Don't tell no one what I told you. Can you get me some food?"

"Where you sleeping?"

"In the basement. That old super so drunk most of the time he don't even know I'm here."

"But it's nasty down there."

"I know. But I ain't going back to that foster home. I can make it on my own. Could you get me some food? And don't tell nobody. Especially them old simple twins you hang out with."

"Okay," I said. "I'll try to get you something. But it's gonna be hard sneaking food out my mother's house."

"You can do it. You ain't dumb. But don't tell no one. Not even Big Russell."

I felt very sorry for Sherman. I never heard of no one being taken away from their family. I always thought Sherman's mother and father just lived somewhere else.

Sherman went back in the basement. I looked over to my stoop. Big Russell, Amir and some other boys was still there. I knew Russell was gonna bother me because of Dotty. But I figured I'd be like Amir and just face what was coming.

When I got to the stoop Big Russell says, "Look at Long Tall Sally. You better tell that little tack-head Dotty I'm gonna get her for what she said."

I ignored him and went upstairs. Mama was in the kitchen like always. "I was just getting ready to call you in," she said. There was no way I could sneak food out. I sat at the table.

"Ma, down in the basement at 130 there's a cat just had kittens. They hungry."

"You always messing with some stray animals. You can't bring no cats in here."

"I just want to feed them."

"We ain't got no cat food."

"Give me a sandwich then."

"If you don't get out of here with your nonsense. Here, take a bowl of milk." She put some milk in an old plastic bowl.

"Can I have some crackers?"

"Crackers? You just want them crackers for yourself. You ain't even had dinner yet."

31

"No, Ma, it's for the cats. You know them old alley cats eat anything."

"Just hurry back from them cats. We can hardly afford to feed ourselves."

She turned to the stove and I grabbed some crackers and an orange. She'd fuss if she saw me, but she was always giving somebody food. One time Mrs. Grant, our neighbor with five children, asked her for two slices of bread and she gave her the whole loaf. My father got mad about that.

When I got outside all the other boys was gone and only Amir was there. "Where you going?" he asked.

"To feed some cats."

"I'll walk you."

"I don't want no company."

"What's the matter with you?"

"Nothing."

"Where's the cats?" he asked.

I know I promised Sherman I wouldn't say nothing, but I couldn't help telling Amir. Somehow it seemed okay to tell him. I'm good at keeping secrets. That's why everybody tells me the gossip, 'cause all I do is listen.

"Amir, can you keep a secret?"

He smiled and nodded his head. We walked over to the basement. When Sherman saw him he yelled, "You big-mouth thing. I knew I shouldn't trust a girl. Why you bring him here?"

"It's okay," I said. "Amir ain't gonna say nothing."

Sherman looked like he wanted to cry. "Why you bring me milk in a bowl? I ain't no cat."

"That's what I told my mother you was."

Amir said, "Sherman, I'll get you a blanket."

Wonder what kind of house he live in where he can just take out blankets, I said to myself.

Sherman stared at me and didn't say anything. I sat on the box with him until Amir came back. He had a blanket stuffed in a shopping bag. Sherman didn't seem so mad now. He went inside the dark, stinking basement and I went home.

I could hardly eat for thinking about Sherman. How was he going to live in that basement?

The next morning I left earlier than usual. I went to 130 and called through the basement window. Sherman came to the door.

"Here's my lunch."

"Thanks. I'm sorry for what I said to you. But please don't tell no one else."

"I won't."

Amir came over also and gave Sherman an apple and a sandwich.

Sherman eating better than me, I thought.

Me and Amir walked to school together.

"He's got to go back. He can't stay in that basement," Amir said.

"Why not? Long as he gets some food. He ain't got no mother or father. I'd die if that happened to me."

"No you wouldn't. Someone take care of you."

"How do you know?"

"I just know."

"You mean you was taken from your family too?"

"In a way."

"But you with them now, right?"

"Well, not my real family. A substitute family."

"A substitute family? That's crazy. I'd do just like

Sherman. Run away and take care of myself. Get my friends to help me."

"He'll get put in one of them homes for runaways."

"It ain't fair, Amir, to take people from their family. That's like slavery. He should do what he wants."

Amir looked at me serious. Finally he said, "Sherman can't keep his family together hiding in that basement."

"How he gonna keep his family together, Amir? He just a kid."

"He could do it. He got to want to do it. And he got to keep himself together, otherwise he can't help them. He keep messing around in the streets he won't be able to do nothing for nobody."

"He can't do nothing for them now. They already all split up and separated."

"Doris, look. When you keep your mind on seeing someone again or being with them, then how can you be split up? You be thinking about them and they be thinking about you."

"That still don't mean you really together, Amir."

"But you are together. Don't you understand? And, see, when you determined that you gonna make something be, you can make it be."

"Amir, you a magic boy or something? How Sherman gonna make it be?"

"He goes back to that foster home. He keep track of where his brothers and sisters be. He make sure they keep track of him. And he just keep thinking about the day when he's able to be on his own and bring them together again. But if he be running the streets, he gonna lose track of where they are. They gonna lose track of him. He'll forget why he was out there in the first place. He may even forget he got a family."

That was the first time I ever heard Amir talk so much. "Amir, you sound like a mother or father."

He laughed. "Doris, we got to make Sherman go back where he supposed to be."

After school I wanted to go see Sherman, but Mickey and Dotty was with me. I think Amir wanted to go see him too, but Yellow Bird and Big Russell was with him.

I got a chance to go around there later and gave him a piece of fruit I snuck out of the house.

That's how it was for a few days. Me sneaking food out the house and running down to the basement when I got a chance. Amir did the same thing. I started getting worried that my mother would begin to miss the pieces of fruit and crackers I took. I could hear her now. "You know we just one step away from welfare."

And Sherman didn't seem right. He looked mean and skinny. And I'm sorry to say this, but he was smelling kind of rank too.

One afternoon we all sat on the stoop of my building. Two big, red-looking policemen came over to us. "Do you kids know a boy named Sherman Shepard?"

"Yes," we said.

"You seen him around here?"

"No," I yelled before anyone had a chance to answer.

Mickey said, "I saw him four days. . . ."

"No, we ain't seen him," I butted in.

"We ain't seen him all week," Amir said.

The policemen looked at each other, shrugged their shoulders and left.

Big Russell said to me and Amir, "Why didn't you tell them we saw him outside the schoolyard last week?"

"Sherman ran away from his grandma and if the police catch him they'll send him to reform school," Amir said.

35

"How you know?" Russell asked.

"He told me."

"How come he talk to you and run from everybody else?"

Amir opened his eyes real wide. "I don't know," he said.

Someone else said, "Well, Sherman got away from that mean grandmother of his. But what happened to his brothers and sisters? They run away too? That's a whole lot of runaways."

Me and Amir looked at each other. "Nothing happened to his brothers and sisters," Amir said. "I saw them yesterday."

Russell stared at Amir like he knew he was lying. "Where you saw them?"

"On the block."

"What time. I was out all day and half the night, my man. I ain't seen nobody from that family."

"Well, it must've been when you went home to eat, or go to the bathroom."

I laughed. Amir sure was slick when he wanted to be.

Russell laughed too. "Amir, with them eyes you could see things no one else is seeing."

Amir just smiled. "You got that right, Russell."

I went upstairs. My mother was in the kitchen so I had to make believe I wanted to feed the cats again.

"Ma, can I have some milk for the cats?"

"Girl, food is too high for me to be feeding them old alley cats. Just give them a little. And this is the last time."

When I got back down everyone had left for the playground. Just Amir was there. We went to 130.

Sherman came to the door. We all sat on an old crate. Amir said, "Sherman, you got to go back to the foster home before you get in trouble. The police was looking for you today."

"You ain't said nothing, did you?"

"No. But you better go back."

"I ain't living with no strangers."

"Are they mean?"

"I don't know. I ain't lived there long enough to find out."

"They might be nice. Some foster families are okay."

"How you know?" I asked Amir.

"I always lived in foster homes."

"You don't have no mother or father either?"

Sherman looked hurt. I was sorry I opened my big mouth.

"No. My mother and father is dead," Amir said.

Sherman said, "Ain't no strangers could be my mother and father. My grandma is my mother and father."

I thought about his grandmother. She looked like she was mean. She never talked to no one. I wondered how he could love her.

"Sherman, you could still visit your grandma," Amir said. "You'll get used to living with a new family. If the people are mean then ask to go to another family."

"I ain't going back."

"Reform school is worse. It's like jail."

"Who's going to look after my grandma? She old and sick."

"We will," Amir said.

Hold it, I thought to myself. I don't know nothing about that old woman.

37

"Come on, Sherman, why don't you go back?"

"How can I live with strangers like that?"

"You just watch them. See how they do. Then you know how to act. Some of them okay."

"What if they ain't right?"

"You tell someone. You get out of there."

"Yeah, you run away."

"No. That ain't gonna do no good. Cops pick you up. Reform school is worse."

"How you know? You been there?" Sherman asked.

"Yes."

I couldn't believe it. Amir in reform school?

Suddenly we see the same two policemen coming down the block. Sherman scooted back in the basement.

"Hide behind the furnace," Amir said.

Then he whispered to me, "Doris, tell Sherman what I told you about keeping his family together."

"Amir, I . . ."

"Don't say nothing now."

Me and Amir sat there.

"Hey, sonny," the cop said, looking at Amir. "You know a boy live around here name Sherman Shepard?"

It was funny how they didn't remember they already talked to Amir earlier. I wondered how anyone could forget his face.

"Yes," Amir answered.

"You seen him around?"

"Yes. I saw him in the park this morning. I'll show you."

Amir walked down the street with the two policemen. Sherman came out the basement and we died laughing.

"Boy, that was close," Sherman said. "Maybe I need to hide out somewhere else for a while."

I was thinking about Amir. "Why don't you go back to that foster home."

"No! I ain't going back there!"

"But, Sherman, you know, like Amir was saying. . . ."

"Doris, don't tell me about what Amir be saying— I AIN'T GOING BACK!"

"Amir said you keep messing around in the street you won't be able to do nothing for your family."

"What do he know?"

"I don't know, Sherman. Sometimes he talk kinda weird. But suppose something do happen to you? Sleeping in basements and on roofs. What about your family then?"

His face looked like a piece of material that somebody crumpled up. I said to myself, Sherman, please don't cry. You gonna make me cry too. "You keep running away and your brothers and sisters ain't even gonna know where to find you."

He didn't answer for a long time. He turned his back to me so I couldn't see his face. I felt like I had a lump the size of a baseball in my throat. He sniffled real loud, then he turned around.

"I hate it in that foster home."

"What about your brothers and sisters?"

"I don't know."

"You gonna upset them more when they can't find you 'cause you don't have an address."

"I'll go back, but if I don't like it I'll run again."

Sherman went over to Third Avenue to catch the bus crosstown—back to his foster home. I was glad he went.

But I wasn't happy for long. Mickey and Dotty's mother saw me come out of the basement with Sherman. Her mouth flew open and she grabbed me. "I'm taking you straight to your mother. Fooling around with some boy in the basement. What is this world coming to?"

"But, Mrs. Johnson, I wasn't doing nothing."

She didn't even listen to me.

"I can't let my Mickey and Dotty play with you no more."

You think them twins is angels, I said to myself. That woman pushed me all the way home. She couldn't wait. She started talking before my mother even opened the door. Mama's eyes turned red. Her lips got skinny like a long piece of thread.

"Ma, let me explain."

"It better be good." She was shaking.

"Ma, Sherman ran away 'cause the authorities took him from his grandma and I was giving him food 'cause he was living in the basement and he was hungry and he ain't got no mother or father."

"Why you lie to me telling me you was feeding cats?" she yelled.

"I didn't want him to get in no trouble. Me and Amir was helping him."

"You was down there with two boys?"

I started to cry. "Ma, he ain't got no mother or father. I thought you was suppose to help someone like that."

She sat down and unloosed her fists. "Okay, but you was wrong. You not supposed to help someone hide out. You should tell me."

I couldn't stop crying. "Suppose that happen to me?" I sobbed.

She put her arms around me. I was surprised. "Oh hush, girl. You ain't gonna be put in no home. Nothing gonna happen to me and your daddy. And if it did we got plenty family. You don't have to live with strangers. But don't you ever lie to me like that again. I won't punish you this time because you really hurt for that poor boy."

That nosey Mrs. Johnson left talking about, "You don't know what mess these children can get into."

I got another sermon from my father, about how it's good to help friends, but don't help them do wrong.

I couldn't sleep that night. I tried to imagine how it'd feel to live with strangers. You got to do things their way. Sleep in a strange bed, eat strange food. Look at strange faces.

I kept seeing Amir in reform school eating bread and water like in jail. No mama and no daddy. I rather see my mother mad and evil, and my father lecturing at me and putting me under punishment every day of the year, than not to have no mother or father at all.

·7·

Friends

Mrs. Johnson must've told Mickey and Dotty the whole story. They asked me a million questions the next day. We got to school late. So we had to stay in. Mickey and Dotty left before I did 'cause I got double punishment for talking in class. All day people asked me questions about what happened to Sherman. I had to write one hundred times "I must not talk in class."

Mrs. Brown finally let me out. My two best friends didn't even bother to wait. But Amir was there. "I waited for you," he said. I was glad. We walked to 163rd Street together.

"Amir, how come you was sent to reform school?"

"When my parents died I went to live with my aunt and uncle. Then I ran away from them."

"At least they was family. Not strangers."

"Sometimes there ain't no difference. They had a lot of children. We all ran wild. Did whatever we wanted to."

"That don't sound so bad to me."

"You get tired of that."

"Why you run away?"

"I went to look for my little brothers and sisters."

"You mean you was like Sherman?"

"Yes. We was separated."

"You found them?"

"No. I just know they live in a big home—upstate somewhere."

"They live with a foster family too?"

"No, they live in a home with a lot of other kids."

"You still miss them?"

"Yes," he said real quietly.

He put his hands in his dungaree pockets, and kicked an old, rusty can into the street. Amir looked so sad. I tried to think of something happy to say.

He turned to me and said, "Let's go visit Sherman's grandmother."

"Nobody goes to visit Sherman's grandmother. I told you that before. We never even went up there when Sherman lived on the block."

"Why?"

"For one thing, Sherman never invited no one up. And another thing, she a nasty old woman."

"We promised him we'd look out for her."

"You promised, not me."

"Maybe we could help her."

"We just kids. What can we do? I almost got in a lot of trouble over Sherman. I ain't messing in nobody's business no more!"

He made his big eyes look real sad.

"Please. Come with me."

"Why don't you ask Big Russell or Bird?"

"I want you to come."

This big-head, big-eyed boy is some pest, I thought.

"You want some protection, huh?" I said. He smiled.

Amir talked me into going with him. After I finished my homework I went back outside and we walked to Sherman's building.

"You do the talking. I ain't staying long either."

We could hardly make out the name on the bell. They lived in apartment 5A. The lights was out on the third floor. We ran real fast to the next landing.

I said, "Amir, suppose that woman run us down the steps with a stick?" He ignored me.

When we got to her door we both just stood there looking at each other.

"You knock," I said. "This was your idea."

Suddenly the door flew open. Sherman's grandma stood there with her crepe-paper face and little squinched eyes. Her body was all bent over. I never saw her so close up before.

"You better get out of here!" she yelled. "What you doing messing at my door?"

I jumped back to the stairs. Amir stood there like he didn't hear.

"Ma'm, we friends of Sherman and we was wondering whether we could do anything for you."

"You liars! You just trying to bother me 'cause you know I'm here alone."

"No, ma'm. We really want to help. We promised our friend we'd look in on you."

"Get out! I'll call the police on you."

"Come on, Amir, let's get out of here."

He stood there. "Can we do anything for you since you're alone? Since Sherman ain't here to help you?"

44

The old lady unsquinched her eyes and looked at Amir for a long time. Amir said, "We in Sherman's class and we was worried about him. Can we help you?"

The old woman's face looked like it was about to fall apart. Then she cried. I was shocked. I'd never seen an old person cry.

"Let's go, Amir," I whispered. He ignored me. Next I felt a lump coming in my throat. I thought old people didn't have tears.

I ran down the stairs. Mickey and Dotty passed by the building as I came out. "What you doing in there?" Mickey asked.

"Nothing."

"What's wrong with you?" she said, looking at me hard.

"Nothing."

I ran to my building. When I got in the house my mother was surprised. "What's wrong with you? I didn't even call you up."

"I have a stomach ache, Ma."

"I told you about eating them greasy French fries at Mr. Sam's store."

I went to my room and stayed there for the rest of the evening. I made believe I didn't feel good. Of course, I had to take some nasty medicine.

I couldn't do nothing but think about Amir and Sherman and Sherman's grandma, and the terrible things that happen to people.

That next morning I didn't wait for Mickey and Dotty. I cut through the playground and sat on the school steps. Hardly anyone was there yet.

Then I saw Amir. I didn't want to speak to him either. I ran to the other side of the yard where no one was. But

Amir ain't got them big eyes for nothing. He spotted me and came over. I thought about how that old lady was crying and Amir trying to be nice and me running like a fool. I couldn't look at him.

"Thank you for coming with me yesterday."

I thought he was teasing me and I got mad. I looked at him, but he was serious. "I didn't do nothing," I said.

"Yes you did. You went with me. Now the old lady knows Sherman got some friends and she got some friends."

I bit my lips. "I'm going there after school to run some errands for her," he said. "You want to come?"

I shook my head yes. He smiled.

"Good, I'll meet you after you come back out," he said. He ran off to the other side of the yard.

I felt better. You know, he never said anything to me or anybody else about how I ran from the old lady's tears.

Me and Amir helped the old lady later that afternoon. We went to the store for her. I still felt a little funny going back over there. She opened the door soon as we knocked. Like she was standing there all day long waiting for us. It was the first time in my life I ever saw Sherman's grandma smile.

And I was shocked at how the apartment looked. She had all these plants. It was like a forest. There was pretty little lacy things on the chairs and the couch. And all kinds of little animals and figures made of glass and wood. And she had pictures of Sherman and all his brothers and sisters.

After that everybody got in on the act. Even that old T.T. helped her with some packages one day.

But me and Amir looked in on her every day. And she wasn't ugly or mean when you got to know her.

46

Like all grown-ups she liked to preach, but she was okay. She always gave us ginger snaps and stories.

Once Mickey was up there with me and Amir. When we left she said, "That's some raggedy furniture she got. No wonder Sherman never invited no one up there."

Me and Amir looked at each other. I felt like telling her the furniture in her house didn't look too new either. "I never noticed the furniture. Guess I was just looking at them pretty plants."

"How you miss that big spring hanging from under the couch?"

Amir said, "What you doing looking under the couch?"

"Yeah," I said. "You just looking for something wrong. At least the house is clean. It ain't right to go to somebody's house and start talking bad about how it looks."

"Doris, you act like you ain't never talked about nobody's house. How about the time you went to Lavinia's and said you saw red rice everywhere."

"It's different with Lavinia. She always talking about people herself. You shouldn't talk about Sherman's grandma."

After that I never asked Mickey to go up there with me. Me and Amir always went there together. Sometimes I'd go there alone. Me and Amir said it was almost like having a grandmother again. Neither one of us had a grandmother or grandfather anymore.

Sometimes I'd be there helping her and I'd think that maybe I could be a nurse when I grew up. I could help old people and sick people.

We also visited Sherman. One Saturday we put our money together and came up with enough carfare for all of us to take the bus crosstown.

He was glad to see us. His foster family didn't turn

47

him in for running away. He said they were okay but he missed his own family. He was glad we was looking out for his grandma, though.

Sherman came to the block the next Saturday and Sunday. But he was different. He didn't sound on nobody or make up names. He didn't even play ball. He was just real quiet.

·8·

The Shooting

"We should get out of school now," Mickey said.

"Yeah. I wish we didn't have to be there until the end of June," I answered.

Dotty said, "I hate May."

"Who's May?" Mickey asked.

"Dummy," I said, "she means the month of May."

"I hate May because it feels like summer, but you still in school," Dotty said.

Mickey pulled my arm. "Let's go to the playground."

I made believe I didn't hear her. I knew I had to go straight home.

Dotty said, "I don't feel like it."

"Well, where you want to go?" Mickey asked.

"To the beach."

Me and Mickey laughed. Dotty could say some crazy things. She knew we only went to the beach once or twice in the summer. And that'd be in July or August. Somebody's father get hold of a car, pile in all the kids in the block and take us to the beach.

"I'll ask my chauffeur to get the limousine and take us all for a ride in the country this afternoon," I said.

Dotty put her hands on her hips and rolled her eyes. "Oh, no. My chauffeur and my limousine could take us."

Suddenly we hear ambulance sirens, and see police cars racing down the street. Then Yellow Bird comes running over to us.

"A boy got shot in the playground," he yelled.

We raced behind Bird. I forgot about going straight home.

There was a bunch of people and police in the playground. A cop came over to us. "You kids live in this neighborhood? Go over there and look at that dead boy. See if you know him."

"What? Dead boy?" we said. My head felt tight. Mickey looked scared. Dotty pushed her way through the crowd. Mickey said, "Go on, Doris. See what happened."

"Why don't you go ahead?" I said.

A cop grabbed my arm and pulled me through the crowd.

"You know him?" he asked.

It was a boy about my age. He just laid there in a patch of dirt, under a scraggly tree. There was no blood, no scars, no holes.

"You know him?" the cop yelled.

I heard Dotty and Bird say, "No. He don't live around here."

I couldn't stop looking. The cop yelled in my ear. "Come on, move it!"

Someone touched my shoulders softly. It was Amir. We left the playground and walked home together.

"Amir, did you see that boy's face?"

"Yes."

"He didn't look hurt or dead."

"I know."

"Amir, I'm sorry I looked. Now I can't forget his face."

We got to my stoop and sat down.

"How was the boy shot?" I asked him.

"Somebody said there was a sniper on a roof. Somebody just shooting off a gun."

"It wasn't no gang fight?"

"No."

"It looked like he was sleeping, Amir."

"I know."

"Why did it happen?"

"I don't know, Doris."

"You think somebody was after him?"

"No. He was just there when the bullet came."

"He was a kid like us, Amir."

"I know."

"Suppose we had been in the playground. I'm scared, Amir. Are you?"

"Yes."

Amir took out a crumpled piece of paper and started writing on it, real fast. First I didn't pay him no mind. I was thinking about that boy laying on that dirty ground where the dogs been. Amir handed me the paper. It wasn't writing. He had made the most beautiful drawing I ever saw. It was a girl with two braids at each side of her face. Tears were falling out her eyes.

"You draw good, Amir. Who is it?"

"You."

I know he was just trying to make me feel good, 'cause

I ain't as pretty as he made the drawing. "The girl is crying. You don't see me crying."

"Well, you look so sad. Maybe you crying inside."

"You can't see what's inside someone."

"Yes you can, if you look long enough."

"Amir, sometimes you talk weird." He laughed.

"Who taught you to draw?" I asked.

"No one. I just look at things real good. Then I draw them."

I looked up at my window. "I better go in now. I don't feel like being under punishment this week."

"Okay, Doris. See you later." Amir was the only person I didn't mind telling I had to be home straight from school. Or that I had to go in the house early.

When I got up one flight of stairs, I ran right into my mother. She was carrying the baby.

"I was so worried," she said. "I was coming to meet you. You heard about that boy?"

"Yes, Mama." I wondered how she knew about it when she was stuck up in the house all day. I was glad I got in before she went out looking for me. That's all I needed was for her to meet me at school like I was five years old.

I couldn't eat dinner that night. The rice tasted like hard little stones. Like those stones in the playground.

My father said, "Guess we don't have to tell you now about that playground."

"No, Daddy."

"I don't want you going anywhere. You stay in front the house," my mother said.

"But Ma, I won't go to the playground. You mean I can't even go round the corner to the candy store, or over to Union Avenue, or. . . ."

"No. Just go to school and come home. And if you must go outside then stay in front the house."

I looked at my father. He looked like he wasn't enjoying his food either. "Your mother's right. Just stay here on the block."

"But that's like being in jail."

"Yes, baby. This is jail. You just didn't know it."

"What do you mean, Daddy? No one is forcing us to stay here."

My parents looked at each other. "Someday when you grow up, you'll understand what we mean. We are forced to stay here."

I couldn't sleep that night. I saw that boy's face on the ceiling—on the wall. I turned the light on and hoped my parents wouldn't wake up. They'd start fussing about the light bill and make me turn it off.

I pulled out the crumpled paper with Amir's drawing. I tried to think about something good—something nice—about Amir.

I went straight home after school was out the next day. I ran into the house and changed to my old dungarees. This way soon as my homework was finished I could go back out.

"Ma, I finished my homework. I'm going out now, okay?"

"Yes. But you stay right in front this house."

When I got downstairs no one was there. I looked up and down the street. Mickey and Dotty wasn't on their stoop either. Everyone is at Mr. Sam's candy store, I thought. I could see Mickey and Dotty fighting over a bag of barbecue potato chips, Russell gobbling up a double scoop of Italian ices.

I looked up to my window and tried to think up a good

excuse for leaving the stoop. There I was, bigger and taller than everyone else and still treated like a baby. I'd feel stupid if Mickey and them came and saw me sitting there. They'd know my mother told me not to leave the block. I figured I may as well go back upstairs. As I was leaving, Amir comes down the street.

"Hey, Doris." He sat down.

"You seen Mickey and Dotty?" I asked.

"Yeah. They in the playground."

"You mean after what happened yesterday they playing in there?"

"The cops found the man who fired the gun," Amir said.

"If I went in that playground, it make me think about that boy."

"I know," Amir said. "I went there with Russell and them, but I left."

"Let's talk about something else," I said. "Where'd you live before you came here, Amir?"

"Brooklyn."

"That's like a foreign country to me. We only go there in the summer when Daddy takes us to Coney Island. You miss your friends?"

"I got new friends now."

"That's not like the real friends you left," I said.

"It ain't hard to make new ones," he said.

"Boy, Amir, I just don't see how you could've been in reform school. It must've been terrible."

"It was lonely. You get used to it."

"How come you so different from the other boys, Amir?"

He laughed. "I'm different?"

"You don't know you different?"

"Why everybody got to be alike, Doris?"

"Well, people laugh at you when you different or strange. Like I hate it because I can't do what Mickey and them be doing. Since that boy's been shot my mother don't want me to be nowhere but in front this house."

"At least you out. Mickey and them ain't doing nothing special."

"They having fun, when I'm stuck up in the house."

"They just be playing 'cause there's nothing else to do. They ain't really having that much fun."

"I'm not like you, Amir. I like to do what my friends do. Like I don't understand why you don't play ball like the other boys."

"I don't play good."

"I thought all boys was good at ball and stuff like that. You ain't ashamed? You don't even try to learn?"

"If I can't play good, so what?"

"But all the other boys play."

"There's a whole lot who don't. They just don't tell nobody."

"They don't want people talking about them and laughing at them," I said.

"People always talking and laughing at somebody. Talk can't hurt you. If you can't do what other people do, so what? Do something else."

"Well, I can't stand for people to talk about me."

"Everybody don't have to be alike. Anyway, Doris, some people like you the way you are."

I looked up the street and saw Mickey and Dotty,

Russell, Bird and the rest of the kids. They came over to the stoop and sat down. Everybody was quiet. "What's wrong with y'all?" I asked.

Russell put his leg over the bannister. "We just got tired of that playground."

Mickey turned to me. "We should've stayed on the block like you and Amir. That playground's spooky."

Yellow Bird was real quiet. Which was strange for him. Then he says, "I was waiting for Russell and Amir after school. Otherwise I would've been in there exactly when it happened."

Amir said, "We all could've been in there."

A roach ran across the step. Russell kept stomping it with his big foot.

T.T. said, "You got him the first time, man."

Then Dotty said, "Somebody did that little boy just like you done that roach."

Everybody looked at her. Dotty could say some crazy things sometimes. But in a way maybe she was right. Except that you was supposed to kill roaches. Otherwise they'd take over the city. Like they already took over 163rd Street. We all sat there quiet. Guess we was thinking about what Dotty said. Then T.T. jumps up and yells, "I'm going to get a wrench and open the fire hydrant."

"Yeah," we said. "Turn on the hydrant."

Yellow Bird jumped in and got his clothes soaking wet. Russell sprayed water on the twins. I was screaming and popping water on T.T.'s head. Even Amir put a can over the hydrant and sprayed passing cars. Then someone looked out the window and yelled at us.

"You kids crazy? Turn off that water. It ain't summer yet."

So we turned off the water and started singing. Mickey and T.T. began. They sounded kind of good. Then Russell did the bass part. I figured there was room for one more, so I jumped into the chorus. Dotty and Yellow Bird danced. Lavinia said, "Bird, you dance like a chicken pecking for worms."

Then T.T. stopped singing. He said, "Doris, you got a good voice."

I smiled. "Thank you, T.T." That was one of my dreams—becoming a famous singer.

"Yeah, you got a real good voice, Doris. Good for calling hogs." Everybody laughed till they cried. I took off my shoe and tried to smack T.T. upside his head. Then Russell tried to hold T.T. so I could hit him. Mickey is singing like she in a opera house. Yellow Bird and Dotty still dancing like they got a hundred-piece band behind them. And Amir was sprawled all over the stoop laughing.

Someone opened their window and screamed down at us again.

"You crazy kids shut up all that noise!"

"No!" we yelled.

I guess we all went a little crazy that day. Crazy from trying not to think about a dead kid that could've been us.

·9·

Changes

After about a week, I guess, people wasn't so scared anymore about what happened to that boy. Even my mother let up a little, and didn't keep me a prisoner of the stoop. But we never found out who the boy was, or whether the person who did it was really caught. There was all kinds of rumors going around. I could still see the boy's face, though. I ain't gonna never forget that.

Me and Mickey and Dotty took the shortcut through the playground to school. We saw this little boy from the fourth grade. Dotty said, "That boy's teeth so big and buck it look like he got a mouth full of Chiclets."

Me and Mickey laughed. T.T. walked by and said, "You girls sound like three witches." Then I saw the spot where that boy was. Mickey said, "What's wrong with you? Don't pay that T.T. no mind."

"I ain't thinking about T.T.," I said.

"What's wrong then?"

"That's where that boy was."

"What boy?"

"Mickey, you forgot already? That boy who was shot."

"Why should I keep thinking about it? I didn't look anyway."

"Girl, you tricked me. You told me to go ahead and you didn't even look. It ain't right to be in here laughing."

"Girl, you crazy," Mickey said.

Dotty walked ahead of us, saying funny things about everyone she saw. But I couldn't laugh. I just hurried out the playground.

When I got to school the first people I saw was Yellow Bird and Big Russell and Amir. They was all excited because Big Russell was going to be voted captain of the team.

We had a special assembly. Hocks grinned so much I thought his big face would crack. Yellow Bird was voted best player. I couldn't believe it. I said to Mickey, "He's going to act simple when we get to class."

"Yeah. He'll probably throw a real basketball instead of paper, now."

But Bird shocked us all. When we went back to class after assembly he was quiet. He answered questions in science and English. We looked at him like he was crazy. Especially since he answered them right. Mrs. Brown was happy.

"I'm proud of your fine behavior today, James." (James was his other name.) "You see, class, it's never too late to improve."

The biggest shock came after school. Me and Mickey and Dotty was in the schoolyard after school watching the boys practice. You know I couldn't stay too long. But I was noticing how Big Russell didn't push Yellow Bird and scream on him like he used to. And Amir was telling them what to do like he was the coach. Suddenly Yellow Bird stops and says, "I got to go to the library to study."

We nearly passed out laughing. Bird studying!

"I'm going to get Mrs. Brown's social studies award."

Russell said, "Bird, you don't know nothing about social studies."

"Yeah, that's when you go out on the ledge," T.T. said.

I looked at Yellow Bird. "He knows the Black history Mrs. Brown gives us. But that's all."

"The Black history part ain't even in them social studies books. Mrs. Brown give us that from her own self," T.T. said.

Bird looked at all of us. "I'm going to study." We passed out again.

"But Bird, it's already the middle of May. You don't even have a book."

"Bird, you still on the Revolution and Mrs. Brown's up to what's happening now."

Yellow Bird grinned. "I'll get some help."

"You beyond help," someone said.

Mickey looked at me. "Mrs. Brown always lets us catch up," she said.

"Mickey, that boy'll have to do social studies twenty-four hours a day to catch up."

"Mrs. Brown says it's never too late."

"It's too late for Bird. Maybe they'll make up a basketball award for him," I said, laughing.

Mickey got serious. "He could take the tests again and maybe he'll pass them this time."

"Mickey, I think you like Yellow Bird. Why don't you

help him?" She tried to hit me but I ran. She caught up with me at the corner. Amir, Russell and Yellow Bird walked ahead of us.

"Mickey, don't it seem funny to see them three boys together?"

"No. I ain't laughing."

"I mean, don't it seem funny to see them three hanging out together? It used to be Russell and Sherman. Now it's Amir, Russell and Yellow Bird."

"Yeah, I guess so. But I don't like what you said about me and Yellow Bird."

"I was just joking," I said.

Mickey put a little sly look on her face. "I think you like Amir," she said.

"I do not!"

"How come you always sitting on the stoop with him and talking?"

"I talk to the other boys too."

"But not as much as you talk to Amir."

I tried to give Mickey a whack upside her head. But she got away. I ran behind her all the way to 163rd Street. When we got to the block, we was surprised to see Sherman standing on the stoop. He had a boy from his new block with him. Big Russell and them was there too.

"I see you girls still running wild," Sherman said.

"We not running wild," I said. "I'm just trying to slap Mickey upside her head, that's all."

Sherman pulled Mickey. "Come here and let Doris knock some sense in you."

Everybody started laughing and talking at once. It was like we used to be.

Sherman was his old conceited self again. He sounded on everybody. Combed his big, fluffy Afro about five times and kept moving around so we could see his new pants. He told Dotty, "Girl, you got dandruff. Look like somebody been planting rice in your corn rows."

Russell laughed in his loud, rowdy way. Sherman looked around for his next victim. I was laughing and easing behind Big Russell's broad back at the same time. I didn't want Sherman picking on me.

Then Sherman yells, "Hey T.T., did you find out yet?"

"Find out what?"

"Where a basketball supposed to go?"

"Russell always be in the way; that's why I can't see the basket, man."

Russell swung at T.T. and I lost my cover. Sherman yelled again.

"Hey, Mickey." I relaxed; he was going to get on Mickey now. I started smiling.

"Mickey, where's stilts?"

Mickey laughed like a fool. "Who you mean? Doris?"

Sherman winked at me. "Doris, you all right girl. Someday the rest of us gonna catch up to you."

"You think you so funny, Sherman," I said.

The only one he didn't tease was Amir. I got mad. I figured I helped Sherman as much as Amir did. He still picking on me, and that new friend of his is there laughing like he knows me. I sat on the stoop.

Sherman posed in the middle of the sidewalk with everyone around him. "I'll catch y'all later," he said.

I ignored him and his new friend. He came over to me. "Lonnie, this is Doris. You know, the girl I was telling you about? She like a sister to me. She helped me out, man. She and that little dude over there with the light bulbs for eyes."

Then he did something that really shocked me. He bent down and kissed me on my forehead. Mickey would have to see.

"OooooWeeee, Amir, you better go get your woman."

Amir smiled at me. I jumped off the stoop and chased Mickey down the block. Sherman hollered after us, "You can catch her, Doris. Just stretch them long legs."

I had to shut that Mickey's mouth. She knew good and well I didn't like Amir for no boyfriend.

The only person he didn't tease was Amir. Sherman just acted like he was real glad to see him. Sherman and his new friend seemed like they was real tight. After that visit we didn't see Sherman much. I guess he rather be with his new friends on his new block.

It seemed like the block changed a little after Sherman moved. Nobody on 163rd Street could think up the insults and names like Sherman did. You be mad when he picked on you. But it'd be real funny when he did it to someone else.

·10·

The Scholar

It was only a month before the end of school. Yellow Bird still tried to catch up so he could win the social studies award. He even played hookey one afternoon so he could stay home and study. He took all of Mrs. Brown's tests over and passed them, but he still had to take the last big exam. We all had to take that one.

When we got home from school Yellow Bird was on my stoop reading his social studies book. We all laughed—except Amir, of course. "Bird, you may as well forget it," Russell said.

"That bird brain of yours can't hold but one fact at a time," said T.T.

Russell laughed. "Bird, let me give you a little quiz. See how much you learned."

"Okay."

"When was the Declaration of Independence signed?"

"1676."

"Oh no, forget it," someone said.

Russell said, "Who was the second president?"

"Abraham Lincoln."

"Bird, you don't know nothing."

"That's the only two presidents them teachers talk about. George Washington and Abraham Lincoln," Bird said. Amir looked like he felt sorry for him. "Bird, I'll help you study for the test," he said.

"See, instead of laughing that's what you should be doing—helping him," I said to Big Russell.

"You laugh at Yellow Bird more than anyone else," Russell answered.

Amir and Yellow Bird went on down the street. We tried to imagine how Amir could help him.

Russell said, "Yellow Bird gonna drive Amir crazy. That boy played around so much his brain don't work no more."

Later that afternoon me and Mickey and Dotty was sitting on the stoop. Amir and Yellow Bird walked by on their way to the library. Mickey said, "I wonder how Amir get Yellow Bird to learn anything."

"Sure wish I knew."

"Let's go to the library and see what they do," Mickey said.

"I ain't going to no library," Dotty said.

"Me neither. You go."

"Come on, Doris. It'll be funny."

I laughed. "I still think you like Yellow Bird."

Dotty started laughing too. "Yellow Bird and Black Bird," she said.

"Y'all so silly." Mickey made believe she was mad. Then she said to me, "I know you like that bubble-eyed Amir."

Me and Dotty was still laughing. Mickey started whining.

"Come on, Doris. Just for a minute."

"Okay, but I ain't staying long."

Dotty ran ahead of us, down the street. "I'm going to

get me a sour pickle at Mr. Sam's," she yelled.

I felt silly going to the library to see how somebody studies. But it was a boring afternoon and at least we'd have a good laugh.

Amir and Yellow Bird sat by the window way off in a corner. We didn't go over there at first. We made believe we was looking for books. Yellow Bird was hunched over a book and Amir watched him. Then Amir looked around and saw us. I waved and opened my eyes in surprise, like I didn't see them before. Me and Mickey walked over and sat down. Yellow Bird said, "Okay, Amir, ask me them questions again." His little face looked worried and frowned up. His hands shook a little. I never saw Yellow Bird like that before.

Amir talked to him real quiet. "Bird, you getting them dates mixed up, man. First remember what happened. Then we get to the dates."

"Okay, Amir. Let's go over it again."

He still got everything mixed up and wrong. Mickey giggled. I made believe I didn't hear her. Even Amir looked worried. Bird looked like he was about to cry. I wondered why he played the fool all this time and now he wants to be a scholar. We sat there trying to figure out how to help Yellow Bird.

Then Amir says, "Doris, I got a idea. Since Yellow Bird remembers that Black history perfectly, he could use the Black history facts to help him remember the other stuff."

"What you mean, Amir?"

"Look, he remembers that the first Black people came here in 1619, then he can remember that one year later the Pilgrims came. One year from 1619 is 1620. The Pilgrims landed in 1620."

66

"Oh yeah, I see. And you know I can write down all the important dates and things that happened. He can study them from the paper later on."

"Yeah, that's good," Amir said. "Then he won't get so mixed up trying to memorize the whole book."

We got so busy helping Yellow Bird, I forgot Mickey was there. She just sat and didn't say nothing.

Bird closed his eyes. "The Pilgrims landed at Plymouth Rock in 1620. The Declaration of Independence was signed in uh, in uh, in 1776. The Emancipation Proclamation was signed in uh, in uh, in 1862. The Civil War ended, 1865."

"He got them right!" I yelled.

That little, skinny librarian looked over at me. Poor Bird was sweating. He should get that award just for trying so hard, I said to myself. I didn't feel like laughing at Bird anymore. I wanted him to win the award.

When we left the library, Yellow Bird's silliness came down on him again. He and Mickey walked ahead of us hitting at each other like two kids. Me and Amir walked behind them. All I did was shake my head. Mickey and Bird made a nice, silly couple.

Three days after that time in the library, we took Mrs. Brown's last test. Most of us just wanted to pass so we could get a good grade in social studies. But Yellow Bird needed to pass with a very high mark to win the award. There was three other students in the class with real high marks. He'd have to beat them to win the award.

When the test was over we went crazy. Mrs. Brown kept us in, but who cared? It was June at last and summer waited for us.

·11·

No More Books

The last day of school and all we talked about was what we was gonna do over the summer. Like we was gonna do something new. Now the summer sounds began: The tinkly music on the ice cream trucks; the crack of the stick on the sidewalk when the boys played ball; girls jumping double-dutch or standing on the stoop trying to sing. Skates and bicycles grating down the street. Now I could stay out a little later. And no more homework! You know I was happy to see this day.

Mrs. Brown always gave her class a party and their awards on the last day. People acted like they didn't care, but everybody was proud to get one. Everybody had on their Sunday school clothes. Even Mrs. Brown had a Sunday-looking dress.

"Well, children, you look lovely this morning. I wish I could give all of you an award, but some of you didn't try at all."

Seemed like she looked straight at me. I turned to Mickey.

"Who she talking to?"

"Those of you who didn't make it this year will have a chance to make up for it in the fall."

I wondered if that meant some of us was left back?

"Now for the awards."

My heart beat fast. Suppose I get an award? I made a 95 on an English test once. But I hoped Yellow Bird got his social studies award.

"Science award—Sharon. Art award—Lewis. Mathematics award—Lavinia. English award—Alvin. Social studies award—"

I held my breath and crossed my fingers for Yellow Bird.

"Dorothy."

Russell yelled out loud, "Oh, that's cold!"

Amir turned around and looked at Yellow Bird. Bird jiggled in his chair and grinned like he didn't care. I knew better. The class got noisy.

"I'm not finished, class!" She looked at Yellow Bird. "Now, James, I know you worked hard for that award and you passed all the tests you made up. But Dorothy worked all year and had a higher average.

"However, I have a special gift for you. If you start out in September the way you ended up this June, you'll win many awards next year."

We clapped and Yellow Bird bopped up the aisle to get his gift. He waved the pretty wrapped package like it was a million dollars.

She gave out the report cards. I peeped at it real slow to see if I was promoted. Me, Mickey and Dotty, Russell, Bird and Amir would all be in the same sixth-grade class. We was glad of that.

Well, I didn't get an award, of course. But if Yellow Bird could get a gift from Mrs. Brown, I know I could get an award next year. But in the meantime, summer was here.

After the party we raced out of school. It seemed like this day would never come!

·12·

The Nit Nowns

"What you want to have a double-dutch contest for?"
I asked Mickey.

"For fun."

"I don't feel like it."

"You just don't want it 'cause you don't jump good."

"I can jump."

"But you don't jump good."

"I'll show you. Okay, let's have a contest."

"Don't back out."

"I won't."

Mickey and Dotty made me mad. They think they the
best rope jumpers in the world. I got some of the little
girls on the block to turn for me so I could practice.

I twisted my ankle, tripped, scratched my legs and
scraped my knees. Those little girls started giggling and
I felt like wrapping the rope around their heads. I chased
them away and sat on the stoop rubbing my legs.

71

Amir was across the street watching Russell and them play stickball. When I sat down he came over.

"You had a hard time with that rope, huh?"

"How you know? I thought you was watching the ball game."

"Why you get so upset?"

"I ain't upset. And I wasn't having no hard time. Them girls don't know how to turn."

"It ain't that important. People ain't gonna hate you 'cause you can't jump rope."

"Why don't you mind your business, Amir? You want me to stand around and watch like you do?"

"Sometimes it's more fun watching."

"I like to do the things my friends do."

"If your friends jump off a roof, you going too?"

"You know what I mean, Amir! I'm not like you!"

He shrugged his shoulders and went back across the street. Amir didn't understand.

We decided to just have the contest with the girls on our block. But word got over on Union Avenue, and who of all people but the Nit Nowns decided to enter the contest.

Now the Nit Nowns is five ugly sisters—Charlene and Charlotte, Pauline and Paulette and Baby Claudette. They live on Union Avenue. Baby Claudette is two. She can't say "sit down." She says "nit nown" instead. Ever since then Sherman call the whole family the Nit Nowns. The name stuck.

I've never known any of the girls on 163rd Street to play with them. None of us liked them.

One woman in my building said, "Them children look

like they just reach in a box and put on whatever they pull out. They some scruffy children."

And them Nit Nowns is always chasing someone home. I even heard that Baby Claudette be slapping other babies. I don't believe that, though.

"They'd mess up the whole thing with they ugly selves," Mickey grumbled.

The big problem was who was going to tell them they couldn't be in it. Mickey said, "Well, I can't tell them 'cause I don't talk to people like the Nit Nowns."

I looked at Dotty but that was no use.

I said, "I can't tell them either because if my mama ever caught me talking to them she'd kill me."

Big-mouth Lavinia says, "How your mama gonna see you talking to someone on Union Avenue?"

"She might be passing by."

"You just scared."

"Why don't you tell them, Lavinia?"

"I ain't telling them nothing."

I saw Amir coming up the street. "Hi, Amir," I said loudly. "Could you do us a favor?"

"What?"

"Could you tell the Nit Nowns for us that they can't be in the double-dutch contest?"

"Why?"

" 'Cause nobody bothers with them girls."

"Why?"

" 'Cause they mean and ugly."

"How you know they mean and ugly if you never bother with them?"

"They act mean and anyone can see they ugly."

"They chase people home and is always trying to mess with nice kids like us," Mickey said, putting an innocent look on her face.

"Maybe they just want to play with you. Did you make up rules for being in the contest?"

"Yes. It's only for the girls on 163rd Street."

"Tell them then. But maybe if you let them be in the contest they won't chase you home no more."

"Amir, you scared of them too," I said.

He just smiled and walked up the block.

Mickey said, "Maybe we can tell them it starts at five o'clock and when they get here it'll be over."

"Yeah. I can just see them coming down the street ready for the contest and it's over." We died laughing.

Dotty looked at us. "But what you gonna do when they find out you tricked them?" she asked.

"Let's don't have no contest," I said.

"But everybody is all excited about it. Even Mr. Sam said he'd give free ice cream pops to the winner."

"We got to have the contest. People been practicing like crazy," Mickey said.

Next day I was coming from the store for my mother and passed by the playground. I was sorry I did. I should've went some other way. I saw the Nit Nowns playing on the seesaw. I turned my head and walked fast, hoping they didn't see me. Then I hear, "Hey, wait up." It was Paulette, the biggest one. She ran out the playground.

"We can't wait to be in the contest. What time it start again?"

"Twelve," I said.

"We'll be there. And we gonna win too."

74

"Okay," I said all quiet like.

"Bye. We'll see you Saturday."

Baby Claudette looked up at me. "Bye," she said, waving her little hands.

Well at least they didn't run me home. I was glad no one heard me talking to them.

As the contest day got closer, I got nervouser. Now I wished my mother would make me stay in the house. I even thought about doing something so I could be put under punishment. But the thing was turning into a big block party. Even the grown-ups was looking forward to it. This is gonna be one big mess, I thought. Me falling. And them Nit Nowns messing things up. I was sorry I got mixed up in it.

Mickey and Dotty's mother bought us two new ropes. A lot of the grown-ups said they'd bring food. Lavinia's father said he'd give the winner a prize from the African jewelry he makes. Three of the older girls on the block said they'd be judges. Even old Mrs. Shepard said she'd make a pitcher of Kool-Aid. And the whole block would be there to see me make a fool of myself.

When Saturday came I thought I had a fever.

"Ain't nothing wrong with you, girl," my mother said. "It's just hot out."

All morning I wished for something to happen to keep me in the house. Maybe it'll rain. I looked out the window. There wasn't a cloud in the sky. Not even a half a cloud. I looked down at the stoop. No one was out yet. But I could see myself down there in a couple of hours. Everybody laughing. Me twisted in ropes from my ankles up to my neck. I could get strangled.

"Hey Ma, you could get hurt jumping double-dutch, huh?"

"You could get hurt jumping out of bed if you don't do it right."

I finally had to face it. We went outside. Some of the women was setting up tables for the food. Maybe I'll just stand right here and faint, like they do in those old-time movies, I thought. Then they'll have to carry me upstairs and I can miss the contest. Why was I always in the middle of something dumb?

The stoop filled up like Yankee Stadium. Even all the boys was there. And them boys never paid no mind to us jumping double-dutch until that day. Lavinia was the first to go.

She did her double-dutch twist.

Dotty spun in the ropes and snapped gum like crazy.

Mickey jumped and turned round and round on one foot.

Another girl did some steps that looked like tap dancing to me.

Everybody wanted me to turn for them. If you don't have someone good turn the rope, the jumper gets messed up.

I was miserable, though. Then, my turn to jump came, I felt like I had to go to the bathroom.

"Come on, Doris," Mickey said. "Go on and jump."

People was talking about how good Dotty was, and looking at me. Amir sat there with his head down like he was studying a crack in the sidewalk. I tried to look like I didn't care.

"I changed my mind. I can't jump that good. I'll just turn."

Mickey looked shocked. Someone said, "Okay, but I want Doris to turn for me. No one can turn like her."

"Aw, Doris, come on," Dotty said. "We won't laugh. Try it."

It was funny, I really felt better. "Naw, it's okay. Bring the next jumper on. I'll turn."

I looked over at Amir again. He looked back at me with a smile in his big eyes.

Things went so good and I felt so good I forgot all about the Nit Nowns. We had two more people to go and the Nit Nowns hadn't shown yet.

"Maybe they ain't coming," Mickey said.

But as the last person finished I see them five sisters cutting around the corner, carrying a big tray. Mickey looked at me and made a face.

Lavinia yelled, "The contest is finished."

Amir jumps up with his nervy self and says, "No it ain't. These sisters is in it too."

I was some mad at him. "Amir's mouth getting big as his eyes," I said.

Charlene came over with the tray. "We made some sandwiches for the party."

My mother took them from her. "Oh, isn't this lovely. You some nice girls," she said. Imagine my own mother telling the Nit Nowns they nice.

Next thing I know people coming out with card tables and all kinds of cookies, cold-cuts, potato chips, pretzels, soda and other goodies. And the Nit Nowns is getting ready to jump.

The minute they started I knew who the winner would be—one of them sisters.

Pauline look like she had on special double-dutch

shoes. They must've been turned over in just the right spots. The heels were worn down smooth. Her feet went so fast they looked blurry.

Charlene didn't move nothing but her feet. The rest of her body was stiff and straight. She looked cool and calm. She smiled and jumped.

Charlotte and Paulette jumped together. They held hands and did a double-dutch dance. Everyone cheered.

I was mad. Before they came, little Dotty had a good chance of winning. Now here comes these two Nit Nowns doing something I never seen no one else do before.

As the judges was deciding, I said to Mickey, "Maybe they won't pick those Nit Nowns. Nobody on this block likes them."

The judges got up. "Okay, everybody quiet. The winners are Charlotte and Paulette."

"I knew it, Mickey."

Everybody went over to them like they was special. Mr. Sam brought over some ice cream and more sodas. We had a real party. One lady said to me, "You really know how to snap them ropes with a lot of rhythm."

People started talking about how we was gonna have another 163rd Street block party and double-dutch contest next summer.

The day after the party I was sitting on the stoop making a box out of some ice cream sticks. Mickey comes running over to me.

"We going to Union Avenue so Charlotte and Paulette can show us that double-dutch dance."

"What? You going to play with them raggedy girls?"

"So? They going to teach us that dance. We need you to turn for us."

"How can you play with them?"

"We just going to learn that dance. Come on."

Since Mickey and Dotty was my two best friends and since I was really kind of bored, I went too.

When we got over to Union Avenue, the Nit Nowns was jumping double-dutch. Paulette spun around on one leg. The baby laughed and clapped.

"Look how wild them girls act," I said to Mickey.

"You just jealous," Mickey said.

"No I ain't. I don't care about no double-dutch."

When the Nit Nowns saw us they grinned and waved. I whispered to Mickey. "They acting friendly now, but them girls could turn on us in a minute. Run our butts right back to 163rd Street." Mickey ignored me. Dotty was already in the middle of the ropes acting the fool with Paulette.

"Come on Doris, turn for us," Charlotte said. I tried to smile, but it was hard. Charlotte jumped in the ropes and she and Paulette did their dance. Mickey and Dotty watched, while me and Pauline turned. I got so interested in the dance they made up I forgot about how I didn't like them.

Suddenly I felt something pulling at my shorts. I looked down. Baby Claudette was tugging at me. "Tun, tun," she said. We cracked up. Charlene ran over to her. "Come here Claudette," she said.

I dropped the ropes and picked up the baby. "You too little to turn," I said. "Go on Charlene, you turn. I'll mind the baby for you."

Claudette took my hand. I'd never noticed how cute she was. She had eyes that looked like they was always smiling.

Now Mickey and Charlene was turning while Dotty and Charlotte did the dance. "Hey, Dotty, you look like you getting it," I laughed.

Charlene came back over to me and Baby Claudette. I noticed that she wore the prize necklace. She saw me looking at it.

"This is a beautiful necklace Lavinia's father made," she said.

"Yeah. Maybe we'll have another double-dutch contest and I can win one for turning."

"You want to wear it for a day?"

"No. That's Charlotte's and Paulette's. They won it."

"It's okay. I mean, all of us won it. The four of us made up the dance. We like that with everything. You remember yesterday Pauline had on this belt at the contest? I'm wearing it today. We all own it."

I looked at the belt. But to tell you the truth, I never noticed the belt she wore yesterday. All I saw was her turned-over shoes.

Charlene sat on the steps and I leaned over the bannister and played with Claudette.

"Doris, you want to wear the necklace?"

"I can't do that. You won that necklace; why should anyone else wear it?"

I felt so ashamed about the way I talked about the Nit Nowns. Charlene was so nice and Baby Claudette was cute and friendly. I reached down in my pocket and pulled out the candy I was hiding from Mickey and Dotty and saving for myself.

"You want some candy? Give the rest to your sisters."

"Thanks, Doris. I got to go upstairs now."

"For what?"

"It's my turn to cook. My mother works all day, so we take care of everything. Pauline, come here and get Claudette."

The baby sat down on the steps with a big piece of candy in her mouth and a big smile on her lips. She looked up at me and pulled my hand.

"Nit nown," she said. Everybody laughed.

"Okay Claudette, I'll nit nown with you."

Well we didn't have to worry about the Nit Nowns chasing us home anymore. But you know how it is . . . as soon as one problem gets settled, something else goes wrong.

·13·

Dog Days

Russell, Amir and Yellow Bird was always together. Sherman only came around sometimes now. It seemed like Big Russell wasn't mad all the time like he used to be.

He was planning games. Like he planned a stickball game between the 163rd Street boys and the Union Avenue boys. He planned a volleyball game—boys against girls—for the Gospel Church Sunday School picnic. He got the boys to practice basketball every day so they'd be able to win the school tournament next spring.

Mickey was sure it was Amir putting Big Russell up to all this. But I said, "Mickey, you know nobody can make Big Russell do something if he don't want to do it."

But Amir was always there and he didn't play ball. He'd just be there watching and talking quietly. I couldn't understand how it seemed like he was with them and not with them at the same time.

He didn't even play the games that we all played together in the evening—like hide-and-go-seek, kick-the-can, and hot-and-cold. He'd just be there and it would seem like he was playing, but he wasn't.

The weather was real hot in August—my mother calls them dog days. Sometimes people get crazy when it's hot—especially when there's nothing to do but sit and sweat.

One afternoon it was so hot nobody played anything. We just tried to find a shady spot on the stoop. That's when the mess started.

Mickey said, "Where's Amir today?"

I said, "He the only one got enough sense to stay in the house."

I don't know who, but someone said, "What sense? I hear that boy's dumb. He ain't really our age. He way older."

"How come he was the smartest one in the class?" I said.

"He been left back so many times he knows all the work," Lavinia said.

"That's ridiculous. How you know?"

"I heard."

"I heard the same thing," T.T. said. "That's why he acts like an old man."

"That boy is smarter than all of you put together," I yelled.

I thought Russell and Yellow Bird would defend their friend. All Russell said was, "Yeah. He's a little strange."

"Russell, I thought you was his friend."

He didn't say anything. Then I said, "Just 'cause he don't act like everyone else, why that make him dumb?" Then everyone jumped down my throat.

"You like him," they said.

"You sweet on little Amir."

Even Russell and Bird laughed and joked. I didn't say anything. I was mad at all of them.

Mickey said, "Ain't he a little too short for you? Y'all look like the odd couple."

"Well, that's better than looking like Mickey Mouse's mama," I yelled.

Everyone cracked up. She couldn't think of a good comeback, so she got mad at me. People get mad easy in the summer. When it's over you never have the same friends you started out with. After that, Mickey and Dotty stopped speaking to me.

One day I'm gonna find out how a rumor starts. No one ever knows the one who said anything. It was always told by someone else. Now, I ain't saying they started the stories, but after Mickey and Dotty stopped speaking to me a second rumor started. That me and Amir was boyfriend and girlfriend. If my mother and father heard such a thing, I'd be in the house the rest of the summer.

I was sitting on the fire escape one afternoon watching everyone outside. Ma came over to me.

"What's wrong with you? You sick?"

"Nothing's wrong. It's too hot out there."

"It ain't cool on the fire escape."

I didn't want her asking me a lot of questions or pouring some nasty medicine down my throat, so I went outside. When I got to the stoop Mickey yelled, "There's the giant. I wonder where's shorty."

I ignored her and went down the street. I couldn't play with the Nit Nowns because they was on my block playing potsy with Mickey and Dotty. So I went to the library.

It was quiet and cool. I sat there and read a book for a while. I wanted to take it out but I didn't want Mickey and them to see me coming down the block with a book. Then they'd know I ain't had nowhere to go but to the library. But then I couldn't stay too long 'cause Ma would think I was hanging out in the playground. And I'd have to spend the rest of my life on the stoop.

I left and started thinking about how I could make some new and exciting friends. As I walked down the block I saw Amir.

"Where's your good friends?" I asked.

He smiled. "I don't know."

"They ain't real friends, you know."

"Why?"

"They talk about you."

"Shows they care."

"I ain't talking to none of them or bothering with them."

"You been staying in the house?"

"Yes. But I see you still be with them. You should hear how they talk about you. You want to know what they say?"

"No. I don't care."

"I do. They saying you dumb. And you way older than us. And all kinds of things."

He looked sad. I was sorry I told him. My father once told me to think before I talk. "Amir, I'm sorry. But I got mad when they said that junk."

He stopped walking and climbed up the big rock in the Franklin Avenue lot. I followed him. He didn't look at me when he talked.

"I am older than you and the others. I'm twelve. Be thirteen in October. I been in so many different foster homes I never stayed in one school for too long. My records never came from my other schools."

"How come they keep changing your homes?"

"Things happen. The people get tired of you. Or they move to another city and can't take you. Or there's something wrong. The authorities take you out that home and put you in another one."

"How does it feel to keep changing homes? Living with strangers?"

"You get used to it, I guess. You get to see a lot of different kind of people."

"But don't it bother you? Don't you feel scared when you go to a new place? All that changing around?"

"Not anymore. Some of the people is okay. Like there was one old man in a family I lived with. Nobody bothered with him. And nobody bothered with me. So me and the old man became friends.

"I used to go to the store for him. Sit in his room and talk to him. Keep him company. He showed me how to play every card game there is. He used to treat his family so good even though they didn't bother with him. Once I asked him why he was so nice when they was so mean. He said kindness always comes back to you. He told me I'd been a blessing to him. He called me the little gift-giver."

"What he mean by that?"

"I ain't sure. But whenever I worried about my brothers and sisters, he used to say, 'It's gonna be all right. You a good boy. Somebody gonna be good to your brothers and sisters.'"

"Is that why you be with us, Amir?"

"Yes. It's like being with my brothers and sisters

again. And I don't want to get in no gangs. Be in no trouble."

I looked at Amir. He did seem much older with his clean blue shirt and clean neat pants. And I really hoped his brothers and sisters was okay.

"Amir, you don't care what people be saying about you?"

"No. It ain't important."

"Well, the next time I hear them talk about you, I'm. . . ."

"Don't say nothing about what I told you. This is between me and you."

"Well, I ain't going to the Sunday school picnic, and I ain't speaking to none of them again as long as I live on 163rd Street."

"Everybody goes to the picnic. Why you let them run you away? Don't hide in the house."

"I ain't hiding."

"If you know what they say ain't true, don't let it bother you."

"I ain't like you, Amir."

We left the lot. As we walked toward 163rd Street I noticed that Amir wasn't all that much shorter than me. Just a little. Mickey was always exaggerating.

We turned the corner to 163rd Street. I prayed nobody be there to see the two of us walk down the street together. But it seems like the whole block be out when you don't want no one to see you. People who ain't been out all winter or summer was out that day.

I just looked straight ahead like I didn't see nobody. Amir went and stood by the boys who was trying to open the fire hydrant. The stoop was so crowded I almost stepped on someone's hand. I heard Lavinia say, "Can't speak, Miss Stuck-up?"

Next day I went to the library again. I went a different way so Mickey and Dotty think I had some new place to hang out—some new friends. I walked down Franklin Avenue and I see Amir sitting on top of that rock in the lot. He had a pencil and pad.

"What you doing?" I asked.

I climbed the rock. He was drawing. It was a picture of the whole block. And it was beautiful.

"No wonder you always looking at things like you see inside them," I said. He could draw anything.

"Amir, when you start to draw?"

"Every time I went to a new family, I had to study the people hard, so I'd know how to act in that house."

"What does drawing have to do with that?"

"You have to look at something real good to draw it. You have to see how it works. You have to understand it."

"I guess you could draw all them people you ever lived with?"

"Yes."

I started going out every morning after I did my chores and meeting Amir by the rock. He'd show me a little about drawing. It didn't make no difference that Amir was a boy. It was like having a real good friend. Sometimes we'd go to the library and I'd show him the two books about Africa I was always reading. Or we'd just sit on that rock for a while and talk. I could never stay too long, else my mother'd miss me.

Once when we was just sitting on the rock he said, "It was hard when my family broke up. All I could think about was finding my little sisters and brothers."

I tried to think how it would feel if my family got busted up like Amir's or Sherman's. Then he asked me, "What you want to be when you eighteen?"

"I'm gonna be a singer and a dancer, or maybe a model or a nurse or a doctor. I'm gonna leave the Bronx, and travel all over the world."

He looked at me and smiled. "That's nice, Doris."

"What you want to be, Amir?"

"I don't know. I just want to put my family back together again."

·14·

Burdens

I felt good even though I only had one friend now. I just hoped my mother wasn't looking for me because me and Amir stayed in the lot kind of long that day. But soon as I walked in the apartment I knew something was wrong.

I didn't smell no food cooking. It was only two o'clock and Daddy was home. I went into the living room. Mama was crying. My eyes filled like a faucet. I never saw her cry except when Grandma died.

Daddy put his arms around me. "It's okay, sugar."

My mother looked up. I rather hear her yell, scream, and fuss, but I got scared when I saw her cry.

"Mama, what?"

She wiped her eyes. "You go on in the kitchen. Daddy and I got some things to discuss. Don't worry."

"Why can't I hear?"

"You not to worry, sugar, we. . . ."

"Wait," my father said. "Let her hear too. This is a family problem. Sit down. I ain't got no more job. I could get some part-time work till the factory calls me back, but that ain't enough to make ends meet. Your mother could do a little work, but then there won't be no one to look after you and Gerald when she goes and I'm gone too."

My mother said, "Maybe between the unemployment check and if I go to work we could manage."

"We'll manage for one week, and that's all."

"We gonna have to go on welfare," my mother said.

My father is a quiet man. But he balled up his fist and yelled, "I ain't having no social workers coming in here asking me about every crack in the wall. Forget that. I'll work ten part-time jobs. We ain't going on no welfare."

I got real scared. Sherman and them was on welfare. Then they got taken away.

My father had these lines around his mouth. It looked like somebody took a pencil and drew them there. "The other thing we could do is send Doris to stay with your sister for a while," he said.

I jumped out of the chair. "No! I want to stay here! I could take care of Gerald while you work."

My mother looked at me and laughed and cried at the same time.

"Girl, you can't take care of yourself. I have to remind you to do everything."

"I can do better. Please, let me help. I don't want to stay with Aunt Mavis and them." I thought about Sherman and Amir, all separated from their family. "Please, let me help. I don't want to live nowhere but here."

My father looked at me. "So many things could happen to you and Gerald when me and your mother is out. Your aunt got a nice house in Queens. She won't mind."

"I want to stay here." I never could understand what

91

was so great about Mavis's house. Everything was so clean you was afraid to breathe. 'Cause your bad breath might leave a film over some of her precious decorations. You couldn't touch nothing. You couldn't move around. I couldn't even go to the bathroom in her house. It just didn't seem like the right thing to do. And my father know he can't stand her house neither. I heard him say one time that he couldn't understand a house that had no smells in it. That it was like nobody lived there.

My mother said, "See, honey, I could work longer hours if I know I don't have to worry about you and Gerald being here alone."

"Would Gerald go with me too?"

"No, that'd be too much. Gerald could stay with your uncle in Brooklyn."

"No. That's just like Amir and Sherman. You splitting me and Gerald up. If I got to go to Mavis I want my brother to come with me."

My parents was shocked. They just stared at me with their mouths open. I surprised my own self too. Guess I didn't know how much I loved that pesty baby.

"I ain't no baby. I'm ten going on eleven. I could take care of things."

My father said, "She is growing up."

"I always wanted my little girl to enjoy her girlhood. I didn't want to put no burdens on her. She's gonna have them soon enough."

"Ma, please. I'll surprise you."

My father said, "Mrs. Johnson and Mrs. Grant could look in on them to see if everything's okay. It'll only be for a while."

"Ma, please?"

"I hate to see little girls taking care of babies and houses and trying to do a woman's job," my mother said.

"You say she never wants to help. Now she does," my father said. He sounded so tired.

"Daddy, let me mind Gerald. I can. I promise."

My mother looked at me. "Doris, if I don't watch you every second now, you'd be over in that playground running wild. How I'm gonna trust you with the baby?"

"Ma, I promise. I won't go nowhere."

"I'd be worried sick."

"Ma, I'll just stay in the house. You could call me on the phone."

Then my father said, "I don't like my children running loose. Or my wife not being able to mind them 'cause she got to work, to help."

"Ma, Daddy, why don't you just trust me for once?"

They looked at each other. "Well, maybe Mrs. Grant and Mrs. Johnson will keep an eye on them," my father said. "And you won't be gone all day. Maybe we can try it."

Lord, I said to myself, I'm going to have *three* mothers now.

"If Mrs. Grant or Mrs. Johnson say they'll look in on them, then I'll do it," my mother said.

"Okay. And if this arrangement don't work out we'll have to do something else."

The baby came stumbling over to me. He grinned like he knew what we was talking about.

"Mama, you want me to ask Mrs. Johnson and Mrs. Grant now?"

"No, Doris, just wait. Me and your father will ask them."

"So when you gonna start, Ma—tomorrow?"

"You just can't wait to see me leave."

"When Daddy start his part-time jobs?"

"Day after tomorrow."

"You gonna want me to start the dinner and do the food shopping. Maybe I'll go to the laundry in the morning and then buy the food in the afternoon. Then I'll clean the house later."

My mother laughed. "Girl, you go from one extreme to the other. All I want you to do is mind Gerald and keep you and him safe till me and your father get home. You don't have to do nothing else except keep that junky room of yours clean."

Mrs. Grant and Mrs. Johnson said they'd look out for me and Gerald. My mother got a job and I was left alone with the baby.

"Now, Doris, this is Mrs. Fox's number if you need me. It's hot and you don't have to be cooped up in this house. You can take Baby out and sit on the stoop. Now remember, no company."

I ain't got no friends noway—except for Amir, I said to myself.

Then she said, "I made Baby's lunch. All you got to do is feed it to him." Her mouth was all pulled down. Her dimples didn't show. It's funny. I hate it when she's fussing and evil. But that's better than when she's sad and quiet.

Look like soon as Mama left Mrs. Grant was at the door.

"Everything okay, honey? I'll be back later to see how you doing."

I made up the beds. Washed the dishes. Thought

about surprising Mama and starting dinner for her. Dusted the furniture. Mama was gonna be shocked at me.

Baby woke up and I bathed him like I see Mama do. I peeped out the window a couple times. Mickey and them out there running wild.

There was so much water on the floor after I washed the baby I had to scrub the bathroom when I finished. Then while I was doing that, Baby goes on Ma's dresser and puts cold cream all over his self. He had it in his hair, up his nose, in his ears, under his fingernails.

"Boy," I screamed, "look at you!"

Then he started crying. He's yelling and screaming. Then there's a knock on the door.

"Doris, what's going on in there?"

I opened the door.

"It's okay, Mrs. Grant."

"Why is he screaming?" She pushed her fat self through the door. "Have mercy! What's wrong with this child?"

"He got into the cold cream."

"Your mother left you here to watch him. How you let him do that?"

"I was scrubbing the. . . ."

"Come on here, boy. You look like a little grease-ball. Let me put you in the tub."

She grabbed him before I could say anything. But he screamed so loud she had to let him go. She stayed in the bathroom while I cleaned him off. Like I needed her to help me. I was glad when she left.

I cleaned up the dresser. Ran behind Baby. Mama called three times and Daddy called twice. Then I fed

Baby his lunch. Gave him his bottle. And made myself a jelly sandwich. Then I scrubbed the kitchen floor. Of course, Baby played in the dirty water. That boy wouldn't take his nap. I was tired. No wonder Ma be evil when I get in from school. But the dumb thing was that after all that work I forgot to clean my own room.

I could hear the boys playing stickball. And Mickey and them sound like they was jumping rope. Well, I had more important things to do now.

I sat at the living room window. Baby was on my lap and he finally fell asleep. Amir walked by and looked up to the window.

"What happened to you today?"

"I had to take care of Baby for my mother."

"Can you come out now?"

"I could if I wanted to but I'm gonna wait for my mother to get home." I really wanted to go out on the stoop and talk to Amir. I missed the library and the walk with him. Being perfect was hard.

She came in at six o'clock, looking scared. "Everything okay?"

"Of course. Baby's sleeping." I waited for her to say something about how nice I had everything.

"Did Mrs. Grant or Mrs. Johnson come in?"

"Yes."

"So you stayed in all day?"

"Yes."

She threw off her shoes. "Whew, girl, I'm tired. That woman has the funkiest house. Just 'cause they know a maid is coming they make sure you got some mess to clean."

"Mama, don't you see how I got the house?"

"Doris! It's beautiful, honey. Girl, you really surprised me." She hugged me for a long time. I know she ain't noticed the house till I told her, but she ain't hugged me like that since I was little like Baby.

"Last week I couldn't trust you to braid your own hair right. What happened?"

I shrugged my shoulders.

"You can play outside after supper."

"That's okay, Ma."

"What's wrong? You been in the house all day."

"Nothing's wrong. Taking care of Baby and the house just wore me out."

She laughed for the rest of the evening about that. "Now you know how I feel."

Daddy came in real late, about twelve o'clock. He looked tired and sad. I could tell my mother was trying to make him happy. She said, "Our baby girl took care of things wonderful. She got the house sparkling."

"She's growing up," he said with his head down in his plate. "This won't be for long. Things gonna be back to normal soon."

"I hope so," my mother said. "I hate you driving that taxi. There's so many crazy people out there."

"Yeah. Seems like every nut in the city got in my cab tonight."

·15·

Understanding

So they let me take care of Baby and the house. After two days I got tired of staying in. After Baby had his breakfast we'd go out on the stoop.

It was early so no one be out yet except Amir. He sat with me until it was time to go in and fix Baby's lunch. I cleaned the house with Mama while Baby took his nap; when he woke we'd go back out. Everyone be out then. The boys played stickball. Mickey and them jumped rope, played cards and made believe I wasn't there. I watched Baby.

Then that big-mouth Lavinia says, "Let's go to the playground, y'all. We don't have to stay on this boring block like some people."

I stood up. "If you talking about me I'll have you know I can leave this block anytime I want."

Mickey said, "Your mama told you to stay on the stoop and that's where you gonna be." They all laughed.

"How you know what my mama told me? You live in my house?" They walked away. I could go to the playground now, nobody'd know. I took Baby by the hand and started to leave the stoop. Then I sat back down. Like Amir say, why should I worry about what people say? And anyway my parents really need me to watch Baby and take care of the house like I promised. And I didn't like going in that playground anymore no how.

I was glad when Amir came over. He sat on the stoop and showed me some drawings he made. I watched him draw a picture of Baby.

Suddenly we heard one big yelling and screaming. Here comes Mickey, Dotty, Lavinia and the Nit Nowns. They running like King Kong is chasing them. Mickey is screaming, "Ma, they gonna git me!"

Dotty tripped over the curb and landed flat on her backside. Lavinia ran right out of one of her sneakers. She left it laying there in the street. The Nit Nowns climbed over a fence and jumped in a backyard.

I laughed till my stomach hurt. Amir laughed so hard he cried. Big Russell looked like he was rolling down the street. Yellow Bird was behind him screeching. Then the rest of the boys came yelling and running. Some of them ran up on the stoop and into the hallway.

"Y'all better get inside," they said to me and Amir. We was laughing too hard to move. One of the boys said, "They having a gang war. A whole bunch of Skulls came to the playground looking for the Warriors." Me and Amir went in the hall. "They looking for the Warriors, so why you running?" I asked.

"When you see them gangs you best run."

Me and Amir looked at each other and laughed some more. "Them gangs ain't thinking about y'all," I said.

We stayed in the hallway a long time, but no Skulls or anyone else came through the block. After a while everyone came back out. Seems like there really was a gang fight in the playground and Russell and all them got scared. I laughed every time I thought about them fools running and nobody chasing them.

Even though me and Ma was getting along fine I still didn't tell her about the gang fight. She been predicting that for years. I knew she'd say I told you so. But after that even Mickey and all the other girls stayed out the playground.

Daddy didn't get his old job back right away like he thought. So the next week I took care of Baby again. Mama only called once a day. It was funny. Now soon as she came home I went upstairs so we could talk about how both our days was. I'd watch Baby for her while she finished supper. She kept telling me I didn't have to, but I didn't mind. Sometimes I'd go out after supper. One evening before I went back out she said, "Doris, you saved the day."

When I went outside, Mickey and them looked like they wanted to be friends again, but I didn't need no friends—except Amir. Mickey and them was too kiddish for me now. I was doing more important things. I sat there cool and quiet like Amir, while they played kick-the-can and hide-go-seek.

"Amir, you know me and my mama ain't had a argument all week?"

"That's good."

"Why you think that is? Seems like everything I do is right. She ain't evil no more."

"Maybe y'all just looking at each other a little more carefully."

"What? You always talking about looking at things."

"I mean, maybe you understand things about each other better."

"You mean like she's not really evil and mad at me, she just be tired?"

"Yeah. And she knows she can trust you, now."

"Maybe you right, Amir."

The following week Daddy got his job back. He was like his old self again. Mama stopped working.

He said to me and my mother, "We is all we got. Being a family saved us. You remember that, Doris, when you grow up and have your own family. Ain't none of us would've made it if we didn't help each other."

It was funny. I kind of missed taking care of Baby. Mama was surprised when I still helped clean and I came in early so I could mind Gerald for her while she cooked. But one night she said, "What's wrong, Doris? Why don't you play with your friends like you used to?"

"They don't like me and I don't like them."

"You'll make up."

"No. We won't. And I don't want to go to the church picnic."

"Don't be silly. Everybody goes. You'll make up with your friends again. Kids always having arguments over nothing."

"Do I have to go to the picnic?"

"Yes."

"But I don't feel like going through no changes with Mickey and them."

"Girl, life ain't nothing but some changes. And speaking about changes, Doris, Gerald needs another diaper."

We both looked at the baby and laughed. He grinned too, like he understood the joke.

It felt so good to laugh and be happy with Mama again.

·16·

The Picnic

I sat way up in the front of the bus with the grown-ups. Amir went in the back with Russell and them. I couldn't think of a way to get out of going to the picnic. "Why don't you go in the back with your friends?" my mother asked.

"I don't feel like it."

"We gonna have to have a talk when we get home."

People dashed out the bus when we got to the picnic area. Blankets was spread on the ground; big picnic baskets filled with fried chicken, potato salad, salami sandwiches, big jugs of red Kool-Aid. It looked like a volleyball net and a basketball hoop was up by magic. The women spread the goodies on the tables. I dipped my hands in the basket of chicken right away.

I made believe I didn't see Mickey and Dotty playing and carrying on. I walked over by the lake looking for tadpoles like we used to. Usually we took a hike up in the woods. I sat by the lake and heard Lavinia say, "If we see a bear I'm gonna run like crazy." Amir came over to me. "Come on. We're going for a hike."

"No."

"Come on. Nobody's mad at you. Come on."

I heard Mickey yell, "If I see a bear I'm going to sic T.T. on him."

"What's the point of being with people and you ain't talking to them?" I said.

"Come on."

"Okay. But you're the only person I'm talking to." We followed the rest of them up into the woods. Mickey and them made believe I wasn't there, so I acted the same way. Those crazy kids acted like nuts. They hooted like owls and played tag. They walked into trees and stubbed their toes on stones.

Bird hid behind a rock and then jumped in front of Russell and Russell fell into a hole. We laughed. Even me who really wasn't there. T.T. went and climbed up a tree and when Dotty passed under it he threw a stick in front of her. She screamed and ran like she saw a zombie.

Mickey thought she saw a bat. "Don't you know bats only come out at night?" Russell said. They played around for about two hours. Someone said, "We better get back else all the food be gone and we miss the potato sack race."

We turned around and started walking back. Amir said, "You going the wrong way."

"How you know?" Russell said. "I know the way back. I been coming up here for years." So everybody but me and Amir followed Russell.

Amir said to me, "They're walking deeper into the woods."

I didn't know which way to go back. We been in so

103

many different directions. This was Amir's first time up here. Russell been up here many times, like he said.

"Amir, you sure you know the way back? Seems like we been walking a long time."

"I remember passing that big tree over there."

"What big tree?" I said. "All these trees look the same to me."

"That one is all twisted more than the others. Look how the bark has that big knot on it."

"I never noticed that."

"I drew a picture of it while we was sitting down before, resting." He pulled out a piece of paper.

"Did you draw pictures of the whole way we came?"

He laughed. "No, but I remember."

After we walked for a while I got scared again. "Amir, you sure we ain't lost?" Then I recognized the spot where Big Russell fell. Amir stopped walking.

"What you stop for?" I asked. He didn't answer me. He turned around and started walking back where we came from.

"Amir, where you going?"

"Come on, Doris, we got to find them."

"They don't deserve to be found. They should've followed you in the first place." After walking for a while we still didn't see or hear them. I knew the grown-ups was worried and mad now. Even though I hated Mickey and them, I was beginning to worry too.

"Amir, they ain't even here now."

"We'll find them."

"Bet the potato sack race started. Food's gonna all be gone too."

"We'll be back before the food's gone." A twig

104

scratched my leg and a mosquito bit me. I was miserable. "Amir, it's too quiet."

"Wait," he said. Then he stopped like he was listening to something.

"What's wrong?" I asked. Then I heard a low, strange moan.

"What's that?" we both said.

We followed the sound. We walked over by a cleared spot and Mickey and Dotty is sitting there bawling like two infants. I wanted to laugh. They hugged each other and cried like babies. When they saw me and Amir it was like they saw gold. "We so lost. And me and Dotty couldn't walk no more and it seem the more we walk the more we get lost and I shoulda come with you and Amir."

"Where the rest of them?" Amir asked.

"They went up there," she said, pointing toward a hill.

"Did they just leave?"

"Yes."

"I'll call them," I said. "I have a loud voice." I walked over to the hill. "RUSSELL, YELLOW BIRD, LA-VIN-I-A, BIG HOCKS." Seems like everything got real quiet. "BIG HOCKS," I yelled again.

"That'll bring Russell out them woods," Mickey said, wiping her eyes.

Then we heard a crashing through the trees. It was Yellow Bird all wild-eyed. "What happened? We been found?"

Then Russell comes through the woods looking like Smokey the Bear. The rest of them followed.

Mickey said, "Amir found the way back."

Amir didn't say nothing. He just turned around and

started walking. They all followed him. I didn't hear boo from nobody. Who's stupid now, I thought.

I was so happy to see the Nit Nowns. They were the first people we saw when we came out the woods. As we climbed down the hill, I was almost ready to go back in the woods. It looked like the adults was going to attack us. Of course, my ma was the ringleader. After I explained and Mickey cried some more, they stopped fussing.

We missed the sack race, but there was food left. We played a volleyball game—boys against girls. The girls won. Them old boys said we cheated. It turned out to be the best picnic we ever had. And I guess everybody was glad we was all friends again. I never heard anyone say anything about Amir being dumb again.

A couple of days after the picnic, I went outside. I could've looked for Mickey and Dotty, 'cause we was friends again, but I felt like going to the library and talking to Amir like I was doing before. I was there for a long time that day. I felt a tap on my shoulders.

"Young lady, it's closing time. You can take the books out if you wish."

I looked at the librarian. "Well, no, ah, I don't know. Okay. I'll take them out." So what if Mickey and them see me with books? If I want to read that's my business.

Everybody was there when I got back to the block. I sat on the stoop and put the books next to me. Lavinia said, "You can't wait till school starts?" But Dotty picked up one of the books and started reading.

Then it started. Whenever everyone is out and there's nothing to do someone decides to put on a show. Usually the boys sounded on each other, but this time it was between Lavinia and T.T.

Lavinia likes to show off. She said, "T.T., you was so ugly when you was born, the doctors slapped your mother."

"Lavinia, you so skinny if you had one eye you'd look like a needle."

"T.T., your mama uses your head for an ice cream scoop."

It looked like Lavinia was winning. Everyone was laughing, but I knew after a while the whole thing was gonna turn into a real argument. I stood up. "Where you going?" Mickey asked. "This is just getting good."

"I'm going upstairs. My mother's going to call me soon anyway."

·17·

Autumn

Me and Ma was coming back from shopping and ran into Dotty flying down 163rd Street on her skates. It was September and in three days we'd be back in school.

"Where's Mickey?"

"She's upstairs looking for her skates."

"Wait up. I'll get mine." When I came back downstairs Mickey was there with three skates that didn't match. Then Lavinia came with some worn-out-looking skates without a key and tied with a rope. Then the Nit Nowns came with only one pair of skates between the four of them. Yellow Bird came over. "I got some skates I can loan you," he said to them. Yellow Bird came back with some skates that looked like the first pair ever made.

"Boy, I feel like wrapping those skates around your fool head," Pauline said. "How I'm going to wear them old-timey, grandma-looking things?" The skates was the kind you see in the skating rink. The wooden wheels was chipped and the leather looked like a rat been gnawing on them.

"These some good skates," Yellow Bird said.

"You use them then," Pauline answered.

"Okay." Yellow Bird put on those skates and rolled down the street. We followed him, laughing like crazy. Pauline and Paulette had a skate apiece. The other two sisters went home. Said they'd use the skates the next day. People in the street looked at Yellow Bird and laughed. He was a sight! We skated by the playground. Russell and the other boys sat on benches talking.

When Russell saw Yellow Bird he said, "Man, take off them things and let's play some ball."

"Does anyone want to borrow them?" Bird asked.

"Nooooo," we yelled.

The boys went over to the basketball court and Amir stayed on the bench. Russell yelled, "Come on, Amir, we want you to see this new move we got."

A yellow leaf touched my arm as we started back up the street. I don't know why, but the leaf made me feel sad. I was happy to go back to school 'cause I was gonna do real good and surprise everyone. I was even gonna get some awards. But I was sorry the summer was over.

Mickey and them was way up ahead. They was acting so wild and crazy they didn't even miss me. I took off my skates and sat on one of the benches outside the playground.

I looked at the same dead, yellow leaf. Things is always changing, I thought. I imagined how that same leaf looked green and fresh the beginning of the summer.

I got up and started walking.

"Hey, Doris. Wait up!"

"I thought you was watching them play ball, Amir."

"No. I got to tell you something."

109

His big eyes looked so miserable. "What's wrong?"

"I'm leaving."

"What? Where you going?"

"My family, I mean, the people I live with, they moving to California, I think."

"Oh no, that's awful. I mean, it's nice you moving to California, but how we gonna see you again?"

"I'm not going with them."

"Oh, that's good. You could go to California when you grow up."

"But I still won't be here. I'm going upstate. They gonna put me in a group home with other kids."

"With your family?"

"No."

"With another family?"

"No. It's just a home with other kids. They have counselors. I don't want to live with another family. I just want to stay here on 163rd Street. The only family I want is my real brothers and sisters."

I could hardly talk. A big, hard lump started growing in my throat. Amir was my best friend. I was losing my best friend. I felt like crying. I don't mean the kind of crying you see in the movies where the lady cries nice, and pretty tears roll down her pretty face. I felt like crying ugly. I felt like yelling and bawling like baby Gerald does when he's hungry or wet. I felt like rolling from one end of the block to the other. I felt like laying on my back and kicking my legs in the sun's face.

Who was I gonna talk to now? Who could I trust like I trusted Amir? I couldn't remember, anymore, a time when he wasn't here. It was like Amir always lived on 163rd Street. Now he was leaving.

"Doris, don't worry. We still be friends no matter what. You remember what I told you about making things be."

I sniffled and tried to keep my voice sounding normal.

"Amir, maybe you could live with us. My mother and father could be your foster parents. I'll be your foster sister and Baby could be your foster. . . ."

"No, Doris. I don't think your parents could do that."

"Why? I'm going to ask my mother right now. We could make room for you."

"They already made all my plans, Doris."

"So? If my mother and father say they want you to live with us, then the plans will change—right, Amir?"

He put his head down. "Doris, I'm leaving tomorrow. Nothing can change now."

"How come you didn't tell me before?"

"They just told me a few days ago. My foster family's going to drive me upstate tomorrow."

I picked up a empty bottle and threw it. Glass was all over the sidewalk. An old lady looked at me and shook her head. I stuck my tongue out at her.

"What you do that for?" Amir asked.

" 'Cause I wanted to."

"Doris, we still gonna be friends."

"How we gonna be friends when you all the way upstate?"

"I'll write you. I promise. It's not so bad. My brothers and sisters live upstate too. The social worker told me I could see them."

"I hope you be with them again, Amir. You'll really write to me?"

"I promise, Doris."

111

We got up and walked back to 163rd Street. "Russell and them know you leaving?" I asked.

"No, I didn't tell them."

"Why?"

"I don't know. You the only one I told. I didn't want to talk to them about it."

When we got back to the block, Mickey and all the girls was there. Amir went to his building. I didn't feel like talking to nobody, so I started walking in the house.

"Where you going?" Mickey asked.

"Upstairs."

"What's wrong with you?"

"Nothing."

"Look to me like you and your boyfriend had a fight."

The next day I stayed in the house all morning. I didn't want to be outside when Amir left. I went out later in the afternoon. I got tired of my mother asking me what was wrong.

We was all sitting on the stoop. Everybody was talking about going back to school the day after next. I didn't care about school or nothing now. I was just thinking about Amir.

Yellow Bird says to me, "Doris, where's Amir?"

"I don't know. How should I know?"

"Come on, Bird, let's go over to his house and look for him," Russell said. "What's wrong with that dude? We ain't seen him since he left the playground yesterday."

When they left, Mickey said, "How come you don't know where your boyfriend is?" She gave me a sly look.

"Mickey, will you leave me alone?"

"How come you acting so strange, Doris?"

After a while the boys came back.

"We rang his bell and no one answered."

"Ain't nobody there," I said.

"Why you didn't tell us that before?"

"Amir moved," I said.

"What? And he ain't said nothing to us?"

"He couldn't. He was too upset. He asked me to tell you."

Amir didn't say to me out loud that he wanted me to tell them good-bye for him, but I could tell that's what he wanted. I told them the whole story.

When I finished, who of all people, but big, loud-mouth, rough-tough Lavinia starts crying. Russell and the rest of them couldn't say anything. We all sat there looking miserable.

Mrs. Grant walked out on the stoop. "Why you kids look so down in the mouth? I know, y'all don't want to go back to school. All you kids think about is playing." She waddled her fat self down the street.

Russell said, "Sometimes I hate grown-ups. They think they know everything."

T.T. says, "I can't believe that little, funny-looking dude is gone."

"Doris, you think he'll really write us?" Yellow Bird asked.

"I'm sure."

"How you could be so sure?" Russell asked.

"I studied Amir very closely. I understand him. He'll write."

Dotty turned to me. "Well, listen at you. You sound just like Amir."

All we talked about was Amir. We couldn't think of anything else. I couldn't figure out how somebody who didn't play basketball, lodies, hookey, talk about other people, lie, cheat or do anything we did, leave such a big emptiness when he wasn't around. How could somebody, who only smiled and looked like he was always seeing the inside of things, make a bunch like us feel so strange when he wasn't there?

·18·

First Day

Even people you saw all summer looked different the first day of school. Everybody felt new. Some of the teachers looked good too. I couldn't believe I made it to the sixth grade. I decided things was gonna be different this year. I was going to make the honor roll for the first time in my life.

I got to school early. It was funny. I forgot to wait for Mickey and Dotty. I stood around in the schoolyard. I wore my new plaid skirt, so I didn't want to sit on the steps. And instead of them two dumb braids I always wore, I had my whole head braided with colored ribbons running through the braids. It took Dotty almost two hours to braid it the night before. I thought Mama was going to fuss, but all she said was, "Halloween's early this year."

T.T. was the first one to show up. And he looked the way he always did. Frowsy. He came over to me. "Hey, girl. You look mighty pretty today. I like your hair. How do you feel?"

115

"Better than you," I said. He turned to the gate.

"Well, look who don't look like Dumbo no more."

I looked to see who he was talking about. Big Russell walked through the gate. He didn't have on them big overalls he always wore. He had on a pair of gray pants with a sharp crease, a white shirt and a belt around his waist.

Yellow Bird was right behind him. His hair still looked like a rooster's crown. He had on new wool pants, a wool sweater, wool socks and new shoes, even though it was still kind of hot. His mama must've bought him new winter clothes and he couldn't wait to wear them. He had a big notebook and a case full of pencils. I didn't know Yellow Bird knew what a notebook was.

Finally, Mickey and Dotty came. They was dressed exactly alike. They wore red wrap-around skirts, beige blouses, gold hoop earrings and their hair was pulled up in nice little puffs on the tops of their heads.

T.T. said, "Them twins almost look cute today."

I didn't sit in the back with Mickey and Dotty. The teacher let me sit in the front row. Mickey and Dotty never asked to leave the room. Yellow Bird opened his notebook and took out a pencil before the teacher put anything on the board. Russell sat away from his friends too.

Wouldn't Amir be surprised to see this, I thought. I kept looking at the door. I wished that a miracle would happen and Amir would walk in the room. Of course, he didn't.

·19·

A New Day

It's funny how things happen. I been doing real good in school. Made the honor roll. Everyone was shocked—including me. Haven't been under punishment since school started.

Me and Mickey and Dotty ain't as close as we used to be. At first it bothered me. Then instead of getting mad at them, I thought about it a lot. I figure we just don't like the same things anymore.

Dotty still plays with those little fifth-graders and Mickey hangs out with some junior high school girls. She thinks she's grown.

Russell ain't as fat and mean as he used to be. And Yellow Bird got the highest mark on the social studies test!

I still have to go straight home from school and can't play outside late, but that don't bother me anymore either. Like Amir says, you don't have to be doing the same thing everybody else is doing.

But the best thing of all that happened is I just got a letter from Amir.

October 15th

Dear Doris,

How are you? Fine I hope. I'm okay. They keep me busy in this place. I had to take a lot of tests and talk to a lot of different people, like social workers and doctors and a psychiatrist. They keep asking me the same old questions. I always remember the fun we had on 163rd Street. There's a lot of trees and quiet and cleanness here, but I miss the block. The Bronx ain't so bad, Doris.

How is Russell, Bird, the twins and everybody? I'll write them soon. One good thing happened. One of my brothers live near here. Maybe I'll see him sometime.

Do you still let things bother you like you used to? I hope you don't. I think about you all the time, Doris. Please think about me, that way, we're not really separated. Together we'll make things be. When you want something bad you have to keep your mind on it. We not really separated. And we not going to lose track of each other if we don't want to.

Someday we'll live on the same block again.

Forever,
Amir

About the Author

Joyce Hansen is the award-winning and critically acclaimed author of fifteen books for young readers. Four of her books have received a Coretta Scott King Honor Book Award, and six of her books have been named a Notable Children's Trade Book in the Field of Social Studies. She has also received a Carter G. Woodson Honor Book Award, an African Studies Association Award, and a National Parenting Publication Gold Award.

Joyce Hansen grew up in the Bronx, the setting for *The Gift-Giver,* and was a teacher in New York City for many years. She now lives in South Carolina with her husband and writes full-time.